D1528043

Whistling Pines

A Mystery

Dean L. Hovey

Copyright © 2012 Dean L. Hovey
All rights reserved.
ISBN: 1475052545
ISBN 13: 9781475052541

Whistling Pines

A Mystery

Dean L. Hovey

To Frank S. Hovey 1920-2012

Chapter 1

Sunday

"Peter," the receptionist called out as I headed to my office. I circled back to the nook where the receptionist sat behind a desk. Connie, who usually had a sunny smile that lit her face, looked troubled.

"Can you go up to Axel Olson's room?" she asked. "Everyone else is busy and his neighbors are complaining about Tucker's howling."

I did a quick time check and saw that I had more than an hour before I was scheduled to make a batch of popcorn and show the Sunday afternoon movie. "Sure," I said.

I heard Tucker baying frantically and scratching at the door before I arrived at Axel's apartment. I knocked and called Axel's name. That only served to heighten Tucker's anxiety. I knocked a second time, wondering if Axel had gone out and left Tucker home alone. I waited as long as I thought it would take for Axel to hoist himself out of a chair and walk to the door. I tried the knob, but it was locked, so I took out my passkey and opened the door a crack. Tucker stopped baying and jammed his nose into the open crack. He scratched at the edge of the door and whimpered until I lifted him up, all forty five pounds of him, and held him to my chest.

"What's the problem, Tucker?" I asked as I scratched his floppy ears and pushed the door open. He was panting as if he'd run a race and I noticed that something reddish-brown stained his feet.

"Axel, are you home?" I called.

I stepped down the short hallway past Axel's kitchen and bathroom, peeking into each as I passed to make sure it was empty. As I neared the living room Tucker began to whimper.

Axel was lying on the floor in a pool of blood that had apparently leaked from a small hole in his chest. I had an instant flashback to Iraq where I had run to a Hummer that had been upended by a roadside bomb. I again saw the young corporal lying face-up on the dusty road, looking unharmed except for a trickle of blood from the corner of his mouth, but totally dead. I broke out in a sweat. Tucker's whining cleared the image and got me back to the present.

The carpet was dotted with bloody paw prints where Tucker had raced around his master after he'd fallen. I carefully stepped around the blood and put two fingers on Axel's neck, checking for a pulse while Tucker whimpered in my ear and tried to lick my face. Axel's skin was already cool to my touch and there was no pulse. Suspecting suicide, I looked around for a gun but didn't see one. That's when it struck me that Axel had been murdered.

With Tucker securely clamped under my arm, I retreated on roughly the same path that I'd used to enter the room and stood at the door while I dialed 911 on my cell phone. My second call was to the nursing supervisor, who was in the elevator before we ended the call. The third call was to the director, who was rendered speechless by the news of Axel's murder.

I set Tucker down and stood outside Axel's door, awaiting the arrival of Jenny, the nursing supervisor. I was having a hard time wrapping my head around the possibility that Axel had been murdered. Kathy, the director, had once described Axel as, "a demanding resident." I'd found him to be condescending and arrogant, often taking verbal potshots at my efforts to provide recreation for the residents on a shoestring budget. I'd often heard him insult others too. He took apparent joy from making people squirm. I wondered if he'd finally pushed someone too far.

I stared at the thermometer mounted on a rough-hewn timber that supported the portico; it read fifty degrees. I was chilled to the bone and feeling colder than three months ago when the thermometer had shown minus thirty-four. The sharp easterly wind off Lake Superior tugged at my windbreaker and pants even though I was nestled between the building and a large cedar tree. Tucker, a basset hound and St. Bernard mix who looked like a shaggy mop with floppy ears, sat shivering at my feet looking even more forlorn than your average basset, his droopy eyes fixed on me. I stared across the expanse of brown grass that had been packed under a heavy blanket of snow for the previous six months. A soggy black glove, newly exposed by the melting snow, lay near the row of residents' cars. Movement caught my eye and I watched a white plastic shopping bag with a red logo from the convenience store down the road blow past, rolling along like a tumbleweed.

The next to last thing I wanted to do on a miserable Sunday afternoon was freeze my fanny waiting for the Two Harbors police while minding the dog. The only thing worse than this duty was the nursing director's job; Jenny was stationed inside Axel Olson's room to make sure that no one disturbed anything. Actually, it was a crime scene, but I had a hard time thinking in those terms. Considering that Whistling Pines is a senior citizen's assisted-living community with controlled access, it seemed terribly unlikely that it could be a crime scene.

The biggest crime anyone could remember was when Phyllis (Phil) Melson reported someone had stolen her glasses. It turned out that Phil had sat on them and her sister Kathryn (Ole) Olson had delivered them to Blustin Optical for repair. It took two days of searching before Ole delivered the repaired glasses and the mystery was solved.

The whine of a siren grew louder as one of the Two Harbors policemen made his way through the sparse afternoon town traffic. I had a vision of the cop sitting in Judy's Cafe drinking coffee and chatting up the waitress when the radio call told him to investigate a suspicious death at Whistling Pines. Two Harbors is a small town twenty-two miles east of Duluth, strategically located on a railhead that delivers iron ore pellets from Minnesota's Iron Range to the ships that ferry the ore across the Great Lakes to the steel mills on Lake Michigan and Lake Erie. There wasn't much more crime in Two Harbors than there was at Whistling Pines, especially when the summer tourists are gone. The tourists overindulge in the scenery, alcohol, Lake Superior, and the local eateries, which tends to lead to some emergency calls for the ambulance and the police. When the three thousand locals reclaim the town for the nine months between Labor Day and Memorial Day, the population drops by fifty percent and life gets pretty quiet. Most of us actually prefer the cold-weather months to the summer months, or what many of us call "the poor sledding season."

The siren stopped a couple blocks away and the muddy black-and-white squad car eased through the parking lot and pulled under the portico. Len Rentz, the Two Harbors police chief, unfolded himself from the car and nodded to me as he closed the door and adjusted his duty belt, which hung precariously from his bony hips. I'd met Len when I was trying to sort out my life and was considering law enforcement as my future. That was before a tour of duty in Iraq left me with little interest in law enforcement and before I'd found that I really enjoyed working with the elderly. I didn't expect that our paths would collide head-on at my new job as the recreation director for Whistling Pines.

"Peter Rogers, how are you?" Len said, shaking my hand, then bending down to rub Tucker behind the ear. "Tell me that the 911 call was a crank and that there really isn't a dead body inside."

"There's a dead body, Len," I said, leading him into the lobby, with Tucker trotting along on his stubby legs. I held my comments until we passed the crowd of retirees gathered around the reception desk under the stuffed moose head. I led Tucker around the desk to Connie and asked her to keep an eye on him for a while.

Hazel Perkins separated from a group of women gossiping about something and pushed her walker over to confront Len. "Well, if it isn't the police chief. Did someone finally realize that the food here is a crime?" she asked as the other gossips followed behind her.

"No," he replied, patting her on the arm. "We found out that Peter's been running an unlicensed bingo game and I'm here to lock him up."

The ladies laughed as we eased past to the elevator.

"Peter's problem is that his programs always start late. He's just not punctilious," Hazel called out as the elevator dinged and the doors opened.

"Punctilious?" Len asked. "Doesn't that mean overly picky?"

"I'm sure Hazel meant punctual, but got the words confused," I explained as the elevator closed. "I had to delay the start of yesterday's bingo because the kitchen ran out of chocolate cake. There was an uprising until the cooks defrosted some brownies."

Len gave me a skeptical look. "Really," I said. "Desserts are very important."

"Tell me about the dead body."

As the elevator blinked "2" I said, "Axel Olson is dead and I think he was murdered."

"What makes you think it's murder?" Len asked as we watched the floor number change slowly to "3." Everything at Whistling Pines moved slowly, even the elevator.

"The hole in his shirt, the pool of blood on the floor, and I didn't seen any weapon," I replied as the elevator doors slid open.

"Hole in his shirt?" Len asked.

I pointed to my solar plexus as I led him to room 311 and took out my passkey.

Len put a hand on my arm and looked me in the eye. "What have you touched?"

I nodded and unlocked the door. "We had a complaint that Axel's dog was barking. When he didn't answer my knock, I tried the door, which is usually unlocked, then used the passkey to let myself in. When I saw Axel on the floor I backed out and called 911, and then I called the nursing supervisor, who also touched the knob. So we touched the doorknob both coming and going. His dog, Tucker, was racing around like a whirling dervish, tracking blood all over the carpet. I didn't realize that it was a crime scene until I saw Axel."

Len pulled on a pair of purple plastic gloves, then handed me a pair. He opened the door, touching only the knob, and moved past me into the narrow hallway to the bedroom/living room. Jenny, the nursing director (who's also my girlfriend), turned to face us. Her lavender smock with yellow ducklings seemed a little out of place in this death scene.

Len stopped at the edge of the living room and took in the scene. I looked around the room, too, like I was seeing it for the first time. The walls, drapes, and carpet were all beige. The kitchen table was bare except for a deck of cards and a cribbage board; the four chairs were pushed against the table. Everything was orderly, from the pile of mail on the table next to Axel's recliner, to the neatly made bed, to the kitchen countertops that were bare except for a plastic water glass next to the sink. The one exception to the order was an eight-by-ten framed photo that had been knocked from the wall. Tiny shards of broken glass sparkled among the carpet fibers.

"Hey, Jenny," Len said softly. "Mind if I take a look?"

She stepped aside and said, "He's dead. Peter checked for a pulse before he called me and then I double-checked with my stethoscope." She watched Len approach the body, crossed her arms and shivered. "I didn't know what else to do. There wasn't any point in administering CPR."

Len squatted down next to Axel's body, which was lying on its side. Axel was a trim man who had a full head of dark hair that was reportedly helped with Grecian Formula. He was dressed in a yellow golf shirt and khaki pants. Other than the blood, he looked amazingly peaceful.

Len studied the scene for several seconds, taking in details about the body, its position, and the room. Len's skinny frame reminded me that many local teens referred to him as Barney Fife, having watched re-runs of the Andy Griffith Show on Nickelodeon. Len was cool with that view. He took his job seriously and preferred to masquerade as Barney when he was, in fact, a shrewd investigator. He'd solved the few local crimes within hours. We lived in a town that was a snippet from the past, where most people didn't bother to lock their houses and even left their car keys in the ignition so they wouldn't get lost. That carried over to Whistling Pines where it was rare to find a locked room other than the nursing office where medications and emergency equipment were stored.

After a few minutes he stood and shook his head. "The dog really made a mess in here. He left little bloody paw prints all over the place. The crime scene guys will love that."

He motioned for us to follow him out of the room. "I want you to secure this room until the BCA gets here. Peter, can you lock the door and sit here until I can get one of my guys here?"

I looked at my watch. "Um, I've got to start the afternoon movie in about half an hour. It would probably be good to keep the residents occupied as long a possible before the rumor mill starts spinning."

"I'll get one of the aides to make popcorn and get the movie set up," Jenny offered.

"Maybe an aide could stand here, and I could set up the movie," I countered, hoping I wouldn't have to guard Axel's body.

Len was shaking his head. "I think it's best if you stay here, Pete. No need to spread the news around to any more people than necessary."

"Fine," I said, with resignation. "Jenny, will you bring me a chair?"

"I'm sure the sheriff's department heard the call and they'll be here shortly," Len said as he pulled out a dog-eared notebook and started flipping through the pages looking for a phone number. "I'd prefer if the deputies and the coroner didn't traipse all over the crime scene before the crime lab gets here. It's enough of a mess with the dog's paw prints already and they have a tendency to get overexcited and walk on the trace evidence."

Len apparently found the number he was seeking. He pulled out a cell phone and punched in the phone number. It was answered quickly and he said, "This is Len Rentz, the Two Harbors Chief of Police. We have a murder scene and I need a mobile crime lab."

"Jenny," he said, pulling the phone away while he waited for someone else to come on the line. "I assume that you have an emergency contact for Axel."

Jenny nodded. "I've talked to his daughter a couple of times and I think that he has two sons, too. I can get their phone numbers for you."

"Does he have any other regular visitors?"

"Not that I know of," Jenny said, shaking her head. "I've only seen his daughter here once, and I've never met his sons. Axel tended to be a little abrasive. He didn't have many people that you'd call friends."

"I'll contact his children," Len said. "Copy the numbers for me and I'll pick them up on my way out."

I'd never seen Jenny so distracted. She was usually the pert, competent nurse but Axel's death seemed to unnerve her. Her rosy cheeks had drained of color, making her face look ashen against her blonde hair. Len's request for the next-of-kin information was the catalyst she needed to get into motion.

"Sure," she said and quickly darted off. Len and I watched her walk away.

While she waited for the elevator Len looked back to me. "I bet she doesn't get much sleep tonight."

Len's cell phone was on "speaker" and a booming male voice startled us. "This is Special Agent Riker. I understand that you're requesting the mobile lab. Can you give me a little more information?"

"This is Chief Len Rentz, from Two Harbors. We've got a homicide and I run a ten-man show. We're not equipped to handle a forensic murder investigation."

"I've got a couple investigators in the mobile crime lab looking at some burglaries in Eveleth. I think I could have them there after suppertime. Will that work for you, Chief?"

Len chuckled. "I've got no other options, so I guess that'll be fine. Have them call my cell phone." He told the agent.

"Pete, unless you have an objection," Len said, as he folded his cell phone, "I'd like to use you as my inside guy. I'd like you to watch for anyone who's acting strange, and anything that seems out of the ordinary."

I knew where Len was going. I'd been a music major at the University of Minnesota's Duluth campus for two years but I wasn't sure what I wanted to do and was getting burned out from the long hours of practice. I took one criminal justice class because police work seemed a lot more interesting than practicing music. Near the end of the course, each student was assigned a ride-along with a local police officer. Len let me ride with him every night for a week. What I quickly learned was that police work, much like music, was hours of mind-numbing repetition interrupted by a few minutes of adrenaline, like the night we got called to a liquor store robbery and I chased and tackled the robber while Len jogged along behind us. At that point, I decided it was time for a total change of direction. I joined the Navy, became a corpsman and was deployed to Iraq near the end of my enlistment. My time as a corpsman taught me invaluable life lessons, including those that made me sure that I didn't want to re-enlist, pursue a career in medicine, or be a cop. Before the Navy, I'd invested fifteen years of my life in the piano, so I went back to the university and completed my music degree. Every time I see Len, he tries to change my mind, in part because he's thinking about retirement and because he thinks I'm level-headed and that I'd make a pretty good cop.

"I think that you'd be better off with Kathy, the director," I suggested. "She has access to much more than I do, and she's really professional." I'd blurted out the first thing that came to mind, and it really sounded like I was trying to duck out of the responsibility.

"Kathy's not the right person. Her job will be to keep the Whistling Pines name out of the mud, and all else be damned." Len started patting his pockets in an obvious search for something. "I shouldn't have quit smoking. The nicotine gum is fine, but it's just not as satisfying to chew and think as it is to light up a pipe and think."

"So, why me?" I asked as Len popped a piece of nicotine gum out of a plastic bubble.

"I trust you to keep your mouth shut, and to pass along whatever may come up without putting it through a 'What will this look like on the front page of the paper?' filter. Besides that, I still want to convince you to give up the old people's chauffeur job to get your law enforcement license."

"The residents may be a little fuzzy at times, but they don't shoot at me or try to run me down with their cars." I hesitated, remembering an incident earlier in the day. "Sometimes they do try to run me down with their wheelchairs, but unless they're motorized, I can usually dodge them."

Len shook his head and said, "Just keep the riff raff out of Axel's apartment until the BCA gets here, and keep your eyes open. I'll be around here a lot over the next few days. Let's plan to have a daily private chat for a while."

And with that, he was gone, his cell phone held to his ear.

Len hadn't been gone ten minutes when I heard more sirens. The whine had hardly died when two brown-shirted deputies burst through the doorway at the top of the stairs and spied me sitting next to Axel's door. I had a bad feeling.

I recognized both of them from the local eateries. It struck me that they looked like Abbott and Costello, one short and pudgy, the other tall and lean. The lean one was all smiles. He looked at my name badge and put out his hand.

"Pete, I'm Deputy Harris and this is Deputy Barnes." I hear that you're the man who found the body, and that you're keeping civilians out of the crime scene." After shaking hands, Deputy Barnes reached for the doorknob.

When he twisted the knob, it resisted and he stepped back. "It's locked?"

"Len asked me to keep it locked."

"Well, we're here to look at the crime scene. Unlock it."

I could see this was all going downhill fast, but I couldn't find a path out quickly.

"No. Len asked me to keep it locked until the BCA crime lab gets here."

The smiles were gone. "You have a key, right?"

I looked down the hallway and measured my chances at making it to the stairs before they caught me. I figured I could outrun Barnes, but Harris looked like he might've been a sprinter.

"Um, yes."

"Well then, use it," Barnes said.

I started to answer, but the words stuck in my throat. I finally managed to croak out, "No."

"No?" Harris looked incredulous and Barnes was turning red.

"Len told me to keep the riff raff out." As soon as the words were out I wished that there was some way to "unsay" something.

"And we're riff raff?" Barnes asked through clenched teeth. I was tempted to count his heart rate on the vein that was pulsing on his neck.

"Well, it's complicated." I stalled.

"We're bright guys," Barnes said, his voice dripping with sarcasm. "Explain it and we'll try to catch on."

"Len said," I paused and tried to find some words that wouldn't sound as insulting as Len's directive to me. "He said to keep people out so that no one walked all over the trace evidence and screwed up his crime scene." The words tumbled out so fast that I couldn't understand them myself.

Both Barnes and Harris were staring at me in disbelief. I was waiting for Barnes, who was now the shade of an over-cooked beet, to explode. He broke out in laughter.

"That sounds just like something that old codger would say. I'll bet he's around a corner listening to this, just to see if you'd really tell us that." Barnes looked down the hallway to see if he could spot Len.

Harris nodded his assent. "Tell you what, Pete. Open the door and show us where you and Len have already walked and we'll follow your footsteps and approach no closer."

A great weight had been lifted and I saw his proposal as a great compromise. I pulled out the key, unlocked and opened the door.

"No one's been near Axel, er, the deceased, since I checked for a pulse except the nursing supervisor, who checked his vital signs, and Len."

I followed them until they stopped at the end of the short hallway where we stood staring at Axel's body.

"There's a lot of blood spread around on the rug." Barnes noted.

Harris said, "There are a lot of tiny bloody paw prints."

"Actually, Axel's dog was going wild in here when I discovered the body and he spread the blood around a lot. There's a pretty good puddle on his other side," I said.

The deputies looked around the small living area. "Not much out of place other than the picture that fell down," Harris noted.

Barnes nodded. "Sometimes we get to murder scenes and it looks like a bomb went off with upturned furniture and broken dishes."

"Yeah," Harris replied. "Remember that one up in Isabella where it looked like the couple had emptied the cupboards throwing plates and cups at each other?"

Barnes was staring at the dining area that split the living room from the kitchen. "They didn't even upset the cards and cribbage board on the kitchen table. Must have been someone he trusted."

I heard voices in the hall and returned to the sentry position to find a stream of senior citizens trooping down the hall toward me. Tucker was racing for his home, his leash trailing. I scooped up Tucker and walked toward them with my hands in the air. "Sorry, but there is nothing to see and no one is allowed down here unless they're going to their room."

Wanda Peltier, a blue-haired woman with an exaggerated dowager's hump, led the advance, pushing her rolling walker. "We heard that something happened to Axel and there are cops all over the place," she said in her outdoor voice. Wanda always wore brightly colored scarves with floral designs. As always, the colors were carefully matched and her light blue dress looked as if it had just returned from the dry cleaners. Some of the residents wore clothes that were at times a little threadbare, or missing a button, but Wanda's appearance was always impeccable.

"You all know that I can't comment on that," I said. "We have to abide by the HIPAA laws. I'd get fired if I told you anything about Axel's health."

"Screw HIPAA!" The words came from a voice in the back of the pack. The elevator had now disgorged a second load of senior citizens, all but one, female.

"Axel would want us to know what is going on," said Hulda Packer, a slight woman with thick glasses. Like most of the others, she wore a flower-printed dress.

"Hey, what are you cops doing here?" Hazel Perkins asked, pushing her walker down the hallway. I turned as Deputy Barnes closed Axel's apartment.

"Don't be stupid, Hazel," the lone man in the crowd, Wilfred "Bud" Larson, said. "They finally busted Axel."

"Why would they bust Axel?" I asked.

"Everyone knows about Axel," Hazel said. "I'm surprised he's gotten away with it this long."

"Gotten away with what?" Deputy Barnes asked.

Hazel started to comment and then hesitated. "It's not my place to say," she said primly. This seemed terribly out of character because Hazel was the hub of all rumors.

After a moment of consideration she said, "He is a...a philatelist." Her statement was made emphatically. Her heavily creased face took on a look that made it quite clear she was a force to be reckoned with.

I was confused, but Deputy Barnes managed to brave the wrath of Hazel and asked the quintessential question. "Was he dealing in stolen postage stamps?"

"Don't be stupid," Hazel snapped. "Stamps have nothing to do with this mess."

"I think Hazel meant that he is a philanderer," Bud Larson offered in clarification. "Hazel was a schoolteacher, but she sometimes has problems sorting her huge vocabulary."

"Axel is a widower," I replied.

"It hasn't been long enough," Hulda said. "There hasn't been a proper grieving period. Enid's only been dead for two years!" Her dentures clicked with her contemptuous words.

Deputy Harris put his hands up. "That's the end of the show, folks. We're creating a fire hazard and you all have to clear the hallway." He advanced toward the group, shooing them back to the elevator, assisting Hazel with the redirection of her walker.

Once the elevator doors closed on the first group, I retreated to Axel's door with the two deputies. Harris put on his best glare, intimidating the remaining seniors into not looking back at us.

"I think that hell hath no fury like a woman scorned," Barnes suggested as the last person climbed aboard the elevator.

"You mean Hazel?" I asked, somewhat repulsed by the thought of her having an affair with anyone.

"My dad was in a senior apartment building for a while," Barnes said, "and he was quite the Casanova. He said that any man who owned a car, had decent night vision, and didn't smell, was blessed with an endless supply of widows who were willing to pay for restaurant dinners and a glass of Port in their apartment afterwards."

"I think it's going to take awhile to get the mental picture of your father sipping wine with the widow Preston out of my head," Harris said.

"I'll also bet that the nursing supervisor knows what medications Axel's been taking," Harris offered.

"I imagine we'd run up against HIPAA if we didn't have a court order to look at the list," I said, thinking of the training that we'd been given that specifically stated that punishment "up to and including termination" would be given for violation of the federal patient privacy laws.

"I'm sure that the crime lab will dust everything in the apartment," said Harris. "They will know if there are any little blue pills in there. More interesting might be how often he was getting refills."

Barnes was rubbing Tucker behind the ear, eliciting a display of near ecstasy from the dog. Tucker's eyes rolled back as he made a noise that almost sounded like a purr.

"Is this the pup that tracked blood all over the place?" Harris asked.

"Yes," I said. "I could hear him barking when I got out of the elevator. He was frantic when I opened the door. I can't imagine what was going on in his walnut-sized brain, but he knew something was very wrong."

Barnes turned his head and looked at the irregular pattern of white, brown, and black that made up Tucker's wiry coat. "He's the size of a basset hound with the short legs and long ears, but he's got a shaggy coat. What kind of dog is he?"

"Axel said that he was a basset/Saint Bernard mix," I replied. "He told me that Tucker was symbolic of the little guy's triumph over the big guys."

Harris frowned. "I don't see how that's even possible. I could believe a basset and beagle, but a Saint Bernard seems impossible."

Barnes shook his head. "I hope the basset was the dad."

"Now I've got this mental image of a hound standing on a little stool." Harris said as he started to laugh.

Barnes shook his head and said, "That almost cancels out the image of my dad and widow Preston."

Chapter 2

It was nearly 7:00 PM by the time I got home. The hubbub of police, coroner, Bureau of Criminal Apprehension mobile crime lab, deputy sheriffs, and all the Whistling Pines management staff made for a scene of chaos rivaled only by the July 4th parade when Lizzie Patrone's scooter malfunctioned and ran through the trumpet section of the Moose Lake High School marching band. It would've been almost comical if not for the fact that Axel was removed from the building in a hearse while the residents were strategically moved into the dining room for an extended dinner.

The answering machine's light was blinking red when I walked in the door. I hit the speaker button and listened to my mother, Audrey, admonish me for missing our regular Sunday evening phone call, then the recount of her charitable activities for the previous week as I peeled off my coat and hung it on a peg behind the front door. After my father's death, she inherited a trust account that allowed her to pursue pretty much anything that pleased her. Mostly what pleased her was giving her time and money to any group that involved the betterment of Duluth, from the Rose Garden Society to the Committee for the Preservation of Canal Park Architecture, the tourist area near the Duluth lift bridge. We spoke on Sunday evenings, just to stay in touch. I decided that she'd probably vented enough in her two-minute message to last her a week. She really wouldn't want to know that I'd discovered a dead body, so I erased the message and didn't return the call.

I really didn't feel up to cooking supper, so I was pleasantly surprised to find a chicken potpie covered by a relatively thin layer of frost in the back of the freezer. Preheating the oven for the potpie had the dual benefit of preparing dinner and taking the chill off the drafty kitchen in my old house.

I was staring into the refrigerator, trying to identify a beverage that was neither expired nor evolving into a new life form when the doorbell rang. When I opened the door I found an angel and her child. Jenny was standing on the top step with a Culver's Butter Burgers bag in one hand and a twelve-pack of root beer in the other. She'd changed from her duckie smock into a pastel pink jogging suit. It managed to accent all of her many physical attributes. Her blonde hair was tied back in a short ponytail and her round face had the glow of the recent removal of makeup. Her blue eyes lacked their usual twinkle, hinting at the stress she was feeling.

"I didn't feel much like cooking," she said, as she handed me the root beer and pecked me on the cheek. "And I figured that you are probably in worse shape than I am."

Jeremy, Jenny's tow-headed eight-year-old son, pushed past us into the living room. "Pete, why isn't your TV on?" he asked as he pawed through the cushions of my 1960's vintage green couch looking for the remote. He had already peeled off a denim vest. His clothing choices were predictable, a T-shirt with some animated character that I failed to recognize, a pair of blue jeans worn through at the knees, and a pair of black tennis shoes with at least one flagging lace. He shared his mother's light complexion and blue eyes. Jenny told me once that Jeremy's father had been a Norwegian Air Force pilot, temporarily stationed at the Duluth Air Force base. He'd swept her off her feet, but was back in Norway by the time Jenny discovered her pregnancy. A little detective work revealed that his wife and three young children lived just outside Oslo. She'd decided not to disrupt his life and to raise the little blonde boy by herself.

I, on the other hand, am not a suave, handsome Norwegian pilot. But I am unmarried, employed, and considerate. I have the dark hair and blue eyes of my mother's Irish family, and the disposition of my Swedish father who never found any topic or situation so important to him that it deserved an argument. I tend to have a little of a hibernation eating pattern that causes me to pick up a few pounds when food is available, then to shed them when I have to cook for myself. Luckily, they seem to balance out and I manage to keep my weight at 180 pounds, which carries well on my six-foot frame.

"Try the right side of the recliner," I suggested to Jeremy as Jenny carried the bag of hamburgers to the kitchen.

Spotting the potpie box she said, "Please tell me you were planning to throw this in the garbage and got interrupted by the doorbell."

She turned the box around and scraped off the layer of frost. "Pete, how can you even think about eating this? It expired in 2007! Even if it didn't make you sick, it has no remaining nutritional value."

"I was more interested in my growling stomach than the vitamins and minerals," I said in defense of my sorry lifestyle.

"I go back and forth between worrying that you'll come down with scurvy, or that you'll die of food poisoning from eating something that's been incubating in the refrigerator three weeks," she said, gesturing at the kitchen.

My guess is that the kitchen underwent a rehab at some point in history when avocado green was in vogue. The cabinets had been painted a darker shade that was more olive drab, and the floor and countertops had both been covered with the same gold and green linoleum. It all matched the green appliances and the gold Formica table with matching gold vinyl chairs, all of it faded. I bought the house "as is" including the dated furniture.

"Hey, if it isn't moldy and doesn't smell bad, what do I have to worry about?" I asked as I pulled out three daisy-decorated garage-sale plates. I was setting a can of root beer at each place setting.

"Do you have a glass of milk for Jeremy?" Jenny asked.

"Um, not one that will pass the smell test." I gave the refrigerator a furtive look. "What's wrong with root beer?"

"He's a growing boy," she replied.

"Mom, can I eat in here? I don't want to miss this. They're down to the last seven contestants."

Jenny was just about to respond when I waved my arms and stopped her. "That's fine, Jeremy. Just come here and grab a burger and take it with you," I said.

I got a softer version of "the look" as Jeremy grabbed a Butter Burger and a bag of fries. It took him less than 30 seconds to grab his load and be gone.

"What was that all about?" Jenny asked as she unwrapped her burger.

"I need to talk about Axel and I'd prefer to not have the conversation in front of Jeremy," I explained as I squeezed ketchup onto my burger wrapper and dunked a fry. "Hazel came up while I was talking with the deputies and made some accusations about Axel's romantic side."

Jenny pondered that as she ate a bite of burger and swirled a fry in the puddle of ketchup. "I'm not sure that his romantic side had anything to do with his death."

"But you can't say that it didn't with any certainty. Maybe he had a jilted lover who was angry about the attention being paid to another woman. Do you know if Axel was having romantic excursions with other residents?" I asked.

"Is this prurient interest, or is there a purpose to your question?" Jenny hesitated, and then added, "Will I be able to tell the difference?"

I tried to give her my own version of "the look," which was not nearly as effective.

"Len asked me to check around to see if there was anything going on that might be a motive for murder."

"So, you're playing Watson to his Sherlock Holmes?" That brought an image of Basil Rathbone and Nigel Bruce bantering inside Holmes's apartment. Most people thought Watson was only a foil for Holmes' brilliant deductions while, in fact, Arthur Conan Doyle used Watson to ask the leading questions that added breadth to the investigation.

"I don't think I have that sort of relationship with Len. I'm just going to ask a few questions to see if something of interest pops up," I said. "And you have still not answered my question about Axel's philandering."

"It's not philandering when his wife is dead," Jenny replied. "Besides, it's not really any of our business."

We ate in silence for a while. My mind was running through suspects and murder motives and I failed to notice Jenny's silence.

Jenny closed her eyes for a moment. When she opened them they were filled with tears. I gently took her hand and pulled her to me. "I was scared. You left me standing alone in Axel's room when you went to meet Len. I was freaking out. I knew that I was safe, but I couldn't even stand next to the couch out of fear the murderer would reach out and grab my ankle."

We stood up and I held her close as Jeremy listened to the television around the corner. After a few minutes she tipped her head back. "You can be pretty nice to lean on."

I pulled a loose strand of hair back from her face and tucked it behind her ear. Her face was flushed from crying, and I had a sudden urge to take care of her. "Are you going to be okay tonight?"

"Do you think there's a killer roaming around the halls looking for his next victim?" She paused, and then added, "It'll freak me out every time I have to walk into someone's room to give them their medicine."

"I think that the whole place will be crawling with cops. You'll be safer at work than you are at home," I said, holding her close and nuzzling her hair. "Will you be able to sleep tonight?"

"I'll make a cup of chamomile tea and take a couple Benadryl. I'll probably sleep fine." She considered that for a second and then asked, "How about you? Will you sleep?"

"I might commune with a double shot of Jack Daniels before bedtime. I think that Jack and I will do all right tonight." Jack hadn't stopped the nightmares that started in Iraq. Now I feared that one more nightmare had just added itself to the list.

Jenny gathered Jeremy's bag and belongings and herded him to the door. I got a brief goodnight kiss.

"At least tomorrow is your day off," she said. "You can sleep in."

As I watched Jenny's taillights disappear down the street, I wasn't as confident about Jack Daniels holding the answer to the hollow feeling in my chest. I watched the red numerals flash 2:00 AM before I could close my eyes and not see an image of Axel lying on the floor.

Chapter 3

Monday

I woke at 4:00, drenched in sweat. A vision of Axel standing next to my bed had asked me, "Can you find him?"

I lathered my face and started to shave but my hand was shaking and I sliced my chin. I watched the blood trickle through the white shave cream as I gently set the Bic razor next to the faucet. I grabbed the edges of the sink with both hands and stared into my own bloodshot blue eyes in the mirror. "Maybe a couple fingers of Jack Daniels wasn't the best plan, or maybe finding Axel by my bedside is dredging up too many ghosts," I said to the mirror.

Having seen too much death and having escaped the bullets and bombs of Iraq it seemed stupid to be so rattled about Axel's death. I took a deep breath and closed my eyes. "Straighten up, sailor," I said to myself. I brought a vision of Jenny's pretty face into my mind, washing away the swirling images of Iraq and Axel's apartment. My hands were suddenly steady and I finished my shave without another cut.

I stood under the shower and let the water pound the knots out of my shoulders. When the hot water ran out I toweled off and ran a comb through my damp hair. My eyes looked better but my stomach was protesting the greasy supper, the whiskey, and the short night. I started to put on a t-shirt and reconsidered, moving to my usual work outfit of a golf shirt and khaki slacks. It was my day off but I needed to go to Whistling Pines. Axel wanted me to find his killer.

I found a few cans of Mountain Dew in the refrigerator and drank one in three gulps as I reran the vision of Axel by my bed. I knew it was Axel, although I couldn't say that I'd seen his face. What disturbed me more was the question: "Can you find him?" Was his murderer a man? Was my subconscious biased to assume that Axel's killer was a man? Had Axel spoken to me?

I trimmed the mold from a slice of bread and toasted it. I decided that I'd had a nasty nightmare and that Axel's ghost had not been in my bedroom. I smeared the last crusty remnants from a jar of strawberry jam on the toast and popped another Mountain Dew as I tried to formulate a plan for the day. My inclination was that a woman wouldn't kill Axel. It might be relatively easy to assess the feelings of the few male residents and maybe discern possible motives for murder. The visitor list wasn't all that long and it might only take a few inquiries to find out if any of them might've cruised by Axel's apartment, or if any of them might've heard the commotion.

Wired by the caffeine and with somewhat of a plan to march forward, I retrieved my keys from the nightstand. Goosebumps rose on my neck as I passed the side of the bed where I'd dreamed that Axel had been standing. As stupid as that seemed, the response wasn't rational. I dashed for the car as the eastern sky grew pink in the morning twilight.

Mist blew in from Lake Superior as the slightly warmer water met the colder air, creating a patch of fog that quickly enveloped my car. I briefly broke out of the veil of fog as I drove through town. Whistling Pines was close enough to the lake that the fog resumed and grew thicker as I got further from downtown Two Harbors. The building was shrouded in white mist when I turned into the driveway, and there was a surreal moment as a giant version of a log lodge emerged from the fog. The BCA's Winnebago was still sitting in the parking lot, now covered with a layer of dew, and Len's police cruiser sat in a back corner under a birch tree that would be stately when it leafed out in a few weeks, but in the cold spring fog it just looked barren and eerie.

The early rising residents were filing into the dining room when I passed through the reception area on my way to my tiny office. Several of the women from yesterday's hallway incident trooped past in a group and I caught snippets of conversation including a few unkind adjectives preceding Axel's name. One woman with newly permed tight curls peeled herself away from the group.

Virginia "Ginny" Jantzen was a longtime resident who managed to keep abreast of politics and the news. Some of the residents had given up on the news, saying it was either bad or stupid. Not Ginny. She could talk about the political candidates and their scandals. She kept us up with state, county, and local politics and even the current situation in the Middle East. Ginny motioned me over to a quiet spot between the aviary and the lending library.

"Pete, I see that there is a cruise ship sailing the Great Lakes." She put her hand on my arm and smiled up at me as the lovebirds tweeted in the cage behind us. "Since you're the recreation director, I think that it would be a grand outing if we took a cruise some day. Some of the people who came to Stella Ahonen's birthday party were cruising from Erie, Pennsylvania, and back. They caught a day trip up here when the ship docked in Duluth."

"I think a cruise ship might overextend our recreation budget," I replied.

"What about just a dinner cruise? I haven't worn my long dress in several years."

I patted her arm and said, "I think that the Vista Queen Duluth harbor tour is more in our budget, and I think they'll let us come casual."

Ginny sighed. "Maybe I'll wear my long dress to Axel's funeral. It's dark blue and it almost looks like a mourning dress if I wear a strand of pearls with it."

My mind was racing as Ginny stepped away. I hadn't thought about a funeral for Axel. Based on past history, nearly two-thirds of the residents would attend, and at least half would need a ride. Our handicapped-accessible van seats only 16 people, so I'd have to make arrangements for a motor coach to transport the more ambulatory. And I'd have to line up volunteers and staff to assist with the transport and the head counts on each end.

It was going to be a long Monday with no way to separate my day job from the investigative job Len had assigned me.

I was pinning on my nametag when Howard Johnson, tall and lean with a head of snow-white hair, came walking down the hallway. He always carried himself with military bearing and his stride was measured. He wore a neatly pressed yellow shirt under a brown cardigan. His khaki slacks had a sharp crease. Howard was the unofficial "mayor" of Whistling Pines, and was very serious about his "responsibilities" to represent the interests of the residents when speaking with the management and staff.

"Howard, do you have a second?" I called.

"I always have a second for you, Peter," he said, a pleasant smile crossing his face.

"Tell me about Axel."

The smile disappeared. "I don't really have anything to say about Axel."

"Let me guess. You live by the motto, 'If you can't say something good about someone, say nothing.'"

Howard nodded, saying, "I've rarely regretted something I didn't say."

"I understand that you and Axel weren't buddies, but I must've seen you talking to him a few times. What was he like?"

"I wouldn't have pissed on his head if his hair was on fire," Howard said. Immediately his face reddened. "I'm terribly sorry. That was really uncalled for," he said.

"Did something happen between you?"

"Nothing specific, Axel was just a general pain in the posterior."

"Give me an example."

"Well, he was always proud of his Swedish heritage. He belonged to the Sons of Sweden and had a little Swedish flag on his door. The truth was that his family was 'Finlandssvensk,' Swede-Finn, from Finland. His family has probably lived in Finland since Columbus landed in the New World. Worse than that, he claimed that he was some sort of war hero. He had that silly picture of some officer pinning a medal on him in Korea. The rumor around town was that he got a good conduct medal for not contracting a social disease while stationed in Seoul."

He paused and considered his words. "I suppose he may have earned a medal, claiming that he'd fought at the Chosin Reservoir when the Chinese invaded Korea. On the other hand, I've heard that he worked with the Finnish underground when they were allied with the Nazis, although it was never really clear which side he was on. When I was in Europe at the end of the war, I heard that the Finnish Intelligence Service had done things that made the German Gestapo look like schoolyard bullies."

"Oh," was the only immediate response that came to mind. "I don't recall any of that from my history classes."

John Dahlen was passing by and Howard hailed him. "Junior, do you have a second?"

John was a stooped man who used a wheeled walker. He'd always been rather quiet and only spoke to me when directly questioned. He was wheezing by the time he wheeled over to Howard and me. He wore a short goatee stained from the Copenhagen snuff kept inside his lower lip. The stain expanded down to the front of his plaid shirt and stopped just short of his belt, which had been adjusted greatly over the years, showing a half dozen worn holes from the days when his waistline was smaller.

"What do you know about Axel and where he was during the war, Junior?" Howard asked.

"Don't know much," John replied. "I was in the Pacific with the Marines. I heard he was somewhere in Europe."

"He ever talk to you about being in Finland?"

"Not much," John replied. "He mostly liked to remind me about how smart he was and how dumb I was. Someone told him that I'd spent three years as a junior in high school, and that's why they called me Junior. I guess he thought it was funny."

Howard shook his head. "Yeah, that sounds like Axel. He liked to pile on someone who was down, even when he didn't know the whole story." Howard turned to me and explained. "Junior had to drop out of school in '41 when his father got kicked by a horse, then had to quit again in '42 when his brother enlisted in the Army."

"My mother finally gave up and sold the farm in '43. I enlisted, too, and I dropped out for the last time," John said without emotion. "I've been Junior ever since."

"You don't remember anything about Axel?" I asked.

"I didn't say that," Junior replied. "I don't remember anything about him during the war. I remember him in Korea. He was some kind of an intelligence officer who didn't have to wear a uniform. He ran around, acting like a big-a-time big-a-shot. I was a platoon sergeant and he didn't know me from dirt, but I knew about him."

"I heard he got a medal at Chosin," Howard said.

For a second, I thought Junior was going to swallow his chew. Some of it must've gone down the wrong pipe because he started to cough. It took a few seconds for him to catch his breath, and even then he was wheezing, his face bright red.

"Son of a bitch never got a medal at Chosin. I saw him driving a jeep south so fast that he got windburn. Probably never even heard a gunshot, just ran for it when he heard rumors that the Chinese were thinking about coming across the border."

Junior pointed his walker toward the dining room and took a few steps before turning back. "I may have only been a junior, but I wasn't yellow."

Howard watched Junior disappear into the dining room, saying, "Junior certainly wasn't yellow. He was awarded a Silver Star and a Purple Heart on Okinawa, and spent a couple months in a Navy hospital after the war. He stayed on in the Marine Corps Reserve and volunteered for Korea. He was a gunnery sergeant at the Chosin Reservoir when the Chinese overran his platoon. He held a rear guard position while his regiment withdrew. After the cease-fire, one of the guys from his platoon was released from a North Korean POW camp and told the story about Junior firing a machine gun until the barrel melted before he reluctantly pulled back. He was wounded, but kept firing his rifle and made sure that every wounded marine was taken along. Because all the officers in his company had been killed and there was no one over the rank of corporal to corroborate the story, the Marine Corps decided that they couldn't nominate him for the Medal of Honor but he got a Navy Cross."

I could hear the diminutive man wheezing as he pushed his walker away. "Junior seems—"

"Let me tell you something, Peter. It's not the guys who look like John Wayne who are the heroes. I've seen big, strapping guys break into tears and cry for their mothers when they got caught in an artillery barrage. On the other hand, I've seen the mousiest little guys race into withering fire to throw a buddy across their shoulders and run back to cover." Howard tapped his chest. "Heroism is all about heart, and Junior has a lot of heart."

I nodded and stepped away before Howard could see me shaking. The discussion of Junior's feats had me flashing back to Iraq with roadside bombs flipping Humvees and Marines with missing limbs lying in the road. I heard again the panicked voices calling, "Corpsman!" as I raced through the gunfire.

The dining room, with its linen-covered tables, each sporting a single carnation, was abuzz with the sound of voices and clattering dishes. The decor was knotty cedar with huge open timbers across the ceiling. Stuffed deer heads and lake trout, donated by the residents, made the room feel like a hunting lodge. Floor-to-ceiling windows and sliding glass doors looked east. On a clear day, Lake Superior was visible in the distance past a line of white pines. Florie, the only African-American person working in the facility, moved from table to table, making sure the flowers were centered on each table and straightening each tablecloth. I ducked into the kitchen and considered a cup of the "power pot," the chef's special morning coffee. Instead, I took a banana from a fruit bowl that was about to be delivered to the reception area. The smell of frying potatoes, bacon, and vegetable soup mingled into a mélange that wasn't sitting well with the backflips my stomach was doing from last night's Jack Daniels discussion, the morning's Mountain Dew, not to mention the visit from Axel's apparition. I quickly peeled the banana and stuffed it in my mouth, hoping it might stabilize the queasiness.

The kitchen hummed with activity as the wait-staff grabbed platters of Danish pastries and muffins for delivery to the tables. The kitchen staff clattered pots and pans as they cleaned up after breakfast and started preparations for lunch. The cooks moved like the gears of a well-oiled machine, with little wasted motion or conversation. Russell, the dishwasher, was busily scrubbing pots and humming an atonal song. Racks of stainless-steel utensils hung over a row of kettles warming on a huge stove. Across the room, Karla Telker, the baker, clothing and face liberally floured, was pulling dozens of rolls from the oven.

"Pete, you look like shit."

I turned to face whoever was making me aware that the feeling on my insides was being telegraphed to the outside. Angie LaFond, a petite girl whose brown hair was tied up inside a hairnet, was staring at me like she expected an answer.

I opened my mouth, but there really wasn't anything to say except, "Yeah."

Angie was one of the cooks, and her white apron was covered with multi-colored splatters. She carried an odor that reminded me of Brussels sprouts, which made me reach for another banana.

"Did you eat anything for breakfast?" she asked.

"I trimmed the mold off a piece of toast."

"You ate moldy toast?" she asked, shaking her head. "I think that ginger tea and soda crackers might be a better choice than a banana and coffee." Without a wasted motion she put the banana back in the bowl, tapped a cup of hot water from an urn, dropped a tea bag into the cup, and scooped up three cellophane-wrapped packages of soda crackers. She handed them to me and nodded toward the kitchen exit. "Take those out to the patio and sit there for a while."

"Thanks."

"I'm not being kind," she said as she ushered me toward the door. "I don't want you to hurl in my kitchen."

Len was on the far side of the patio, filling the bowl of his pipe with tobacco. The pipe filling was obviously a ritual. He carefully tamped the tobacco and tested the draw before striking a match and slowly inhaling, then blowing a stream of smoke skyward. His uniform was rumpled, like he'd slept in it, and his eyes were drooping with fatigue. He looked up at me, apparently reveling in the nicotine rush.

He watched silently as I ripped the cellophane wrappers off two packs of crackers and stuffed them in my mouth. I was taking a sip of tea when he finally spoke.

"Pete, you look like shit."

"That seems to be the consensus. The cook told me to leave the kitchen before I hurled." I took a sip of tea, hoping to stave off another wave of nausea. "By the way, Barnes and Harris got quite a chuckle out of me telling them that you didn't want them to walk all over the evidence."

The corner of Len's mouth twitched in what might've been a smile. "Harris said he wasn't sure if you were going to wet yourself or run."

"Yeah, it was a treat for all of us. You told me yesterday that you'd stopped smoking," I said eyeing his pipe.

"Yesterday," he replied, "I wasn't trying to solve the first murder in this town since Frenchman Jacque stabbed a guy off an ore boat over the affections of a dancehall girl."

"Have you got any leads?" I asked, unwrapping the last cracker package.

"The murder weapon appears to be a narrow knife, sharp on both edges, like a stiletto." Len drew another drag on the pipe and blew the smoke to the side. "How goes your assignment? Do you have anything for me?" he asked as he pulled out the tobacco tamper and again went through the ceremony of carefully packing the bowl of the pipe before relighting it.

"I'm a little surprised at the resentment that a few of the residents had for Axel, but I doubt that any of it was deep enough to be a murder motive."

"Give me some specifics."

"Well, Howard Johnson didn't seem to have much time for Axel."

Len gave me a "tell me more" motion with his pipe-wielding hand.

"Well, he said that Axel wasn't really a Swede. He pretended to be a Swede, but his family emigrated to Finland when it was a Swedish territory and the whole group became pariahs who were disliked by both the Swedes and the Finns. He also said that he thought Axel might've collaborated with the Nazis. Then Junior Dahlen made a comment like he didn't think that Axel deserved the Korean War medal he always bragged about."

"Interesting," Len said as he tapped the tobacco plug from the pipe into the urn and took out his spiral notebook. "The only thing disturbed in Axel's apartment was the picture of him getting a medal pinned on his chest. It was smashed on the floor. How angry was Howard?" Len asked after scribbling a note.

"Howard is always very proper. He never lost his temper, but he made a derogatory comment that he apologized for as soon as it was out of his mouth."

"The comment about being a Swede-Finn is interesting," Len said, tapping his pen on the table. "Stella Ahonen had a birthday party about the time of Axel's death, and there were an extra 24 or 30 people of Finnish extraction here. I was just tracing down all who had signed in on the guest register. It seems there were at least a dozen more who didn't use the register."

"That's got to be ancient history," I said. "Who would carry a grudge from the 1940s to commit a murder now?"

"You ever hear of the Hatfields and McCoys?" Len asked as he returned the notebook to his pocket. "I think they feuded for two hundred years, and I'm not sure it's over yet," he said, slipping the unlit pipe into his pocket. "Is there anything else?"

"Hazel Packer accused Axel of philandering."

Len choked and then snorted. "You're kidding."

"Deputy Barnes said that his father was quite a Casanova in his nursing home. He suggested that we check Axel's prescriptions for little blue romance pills."

Len tipped his head back and looked at the sky. After a few seconds he shook his head and looked down. "Women use poison. A knife is a man's weapon."

Chapter 4

Amid their normal daily activities, I tried to corner each of the remaining ten or so male residents to assess their feelings about Axel. It was mostly an unsettling exercise in futility, with five of them having short-term memory issues.

Gary "Red" Tschida answered his door with a look of confusion. "Is it Thursday already?" he asked. He still had a full head of hair, which had once been red, garnering his nickname. Now it was mostly white with a brassy undertone. He'd apparently forgotten his morning shave and white whiskers covered his face. He wore a quilted white t-shirt that barely covered his barrel chest and rainbow-colored suspenders that kept his blue jeans from slipping off.

"It's only Monday morning," I replied. "We'll go to Betty's Pies like always on Thursday, but I thought I'd see how you were doing. Lots of the residents are stirred up over Axel's death."

Gary nodded knowingly. "C'mon in and sit. I'm a good listener and you can tell me how you're feeling." After every few words he had to push his upper dentures back into place with his tongue, making a sound like a dog with peanut butter stuck to the roof of his mouth.

Gary's apartment was a small studio apartment like Axel's, with a sliding pocket door dividing the bedroom portion of the apartment from the living room. He had a few clean coffee cups and plates drying in the sink. Whistling Pines had people in a variety of living and dining arrangements. Gary chose to prepare breakfast and lunch for himself and ate his evening meal in the dining room. Others, like Axel, ate every meal in the dining room.

He had a stack of the Styrofoam cups from the cafeteria stacked on the counter. "Um, Gary," I stammered, trying to frame the question properly. "You don't bring those used cups back to the cafeteria, do you?"

"Oh, no, the cafeteria has lots of them. I wash them up and bring them to the food shelf for the workers. They can't afford coffee cups and they really appreciate getting these nice plastic ones."

"How well did you know Axel?" I asked.

"It's a small town, you know," Gary said with a hint of an accent that sounded more like the movie Fargo than any specific ethnicity. "I've probably been bumping into him for decades. I can't really say the exact moment that we met, if that's what you're asking." Gary's smile lit up, "Say, would you like a cup of coffee?"

I looked at the stack of plastic cups with apprehension. "Thanks, but I've had my limit of caffeine for today. Were you and Axel friends?" I asked, trying to steer the conversation back on track.

"Not so much," Gary said, wrinkling his nose as he sat in his recliner. "He was full of himself and liked to talk big about things. I've seen what money he made, and how he made it, and I didn't have much time for his nonsense."

"Nonsense?"

"I've got a lot of respect for people who've worked hard to get ahead. Axel's not on that list of people."

He reached into the side pocket of his recliner and pulled out a stack of papers. "I keep some stuff that interests me," he said. Most were advertisements for hearing aids or old newspaper headlines about the Minnesota Twins. He sorted through the stack and found a newspaper clipping that he passed to me. The headline was, "Landlocked Developer."

The article was only a few paragraphs long and said that a land developer had purchased a prime piece of real estate that overlooked Lake Superior, with plans to build a vacation condo development to bring in vacationers from the Cities. He hit a snag when he tried to build a driveway across the land between his development and the highway. The title to the land stated that there was an agricultural easement. The owner of the blocking property had fought the developer in court and kept him from building a driveway.

I handed the clipping back to Gary and asked, "Does this have something to do with Axel?"

"Axel owns the land the easement crosses."

"So, he's been holding up the development of the landlocked property?"

"He's been keeping a lot of good people from having good paying construction jobs. He's keeping a whole bunch of people from making some money on construction materials. And he's keeping more tourists from coming here and putting money into our local economy."

"I suppose he was getting lots of pressure to sell the property or an easement," I said, thinking about the number of enemies that strategy would make.

"He told me that he'd never considered selling. He was happy just to be a pain in the butt, knowing he was causing an ulcer for this developer who already has a couple hundred thousand dollars spent on building plans, land, and building permits. Axel used to laugh about it."

"Sounds like it could be a murder motive to me," I said, my mind reeling with the number of people who might have been impacted by Axel's intransigence.

"Don't forget his kids," Gary added. "Axel was proud that he never shared a penny with them, and here he sat on a piece of swampy property that could be worth over a hundred thousand dollars to the developer. I'd say that might be motivation to get rid of a dad who spent his whole life making everyone he touches miserable."

"Did anyone else have a motive to kill Axel?"

Gary's eyes twinkled. "I can't remember the year, but if you check the newspapers from deer hunting season in the late sixties, you might find an article about a tragic hunting accident. Axel was part owner of a little bar south of Duluth that wasn't doing very well, and someone mistook his partner for a big buck and shot him dead. Axel hadn't fired his gun, so he wasn't a suspect, but there weren't any other hunters near the two of them. Lucky for Axel, they'd bought business life insurance policies on each other, and Axel collected ten times what the little bar was worth. Pity that the widow hadn't had the foresight to get insurance, too. Of course, her plight wasn't Axel's problem. I heard he got generous and bought three bus tickets to Minneapolis so she could take the kids to live with her sister."

"I have a hard time seeing Axel with lots of money," I said. "If he had the money you're talking about, he could've been living in a fancy house with a housekeeper instead of in a studio apartment here."

"That would be a violation of Axel's first rule: You don't get rich by spending money."

Chapter 5

I hesitated for a half second when I opened Gary's door to leave. I'm not sure if I heard the whine of the electric motors, or if I had a premonition of impending peril, but that hesitation saved me from a collision with two drag racers who flashed past the door, nearly running over the toes of my shoes.

"Look out, Pete!" Elton Neilson yelled a second after he'd passed driving his blue "Hurricane" electric scooter. Elton owned Neilson Brothers clothing store, and had never been seen in anything but a suit. The residents often commented that he even wore a suit and Florsheim shoes when he cut his grass.

Half a length behind him was "Scooter" Arneson, dressed in "Dickie" blue work pants and a Minnesota Twins sweatshirt. He was racing his red "Victor" scooter, painted with yellow flames, and losing ground the further they got down the hallway. Scooter had been a legendary hot-rod racer and heavy drinker. He'd reportedly called the fire chief at home late one evening to announce that his supper was on fire. When the fire chief asked why Scooter hadn't dialed 911, he responded that he thought that maybe the chief could bring over a "squirt hose" and take care of it without waking up all the volunteers.

"GUYS! Stop before you kill someone," I yelled after them.

Scooter slowed and just missed colliding with a small table that a vase and flowers were still wobbling on after the close call, "I want a rematch," he yelled at Elton, who'd disappeared around the corner.

"Hey, Scooter," I said, catching up with him before he could continue his chase. "Hold up for a second."

"I was just getting my scooter into the steep part of the power curve. Another fifty feet and I would've left him in my dust."

"I don't think you guys should be racing in the hallways. Someone's going to get hurt."

"Pete, you're such a killjoy."

"I was just talking to Gary Tschida and he had some pretty sad stories about Axel and things that he'd done to people."

"Red worries about that kind of stuff. I didn't spend much time dwelling on it. It tended to make me sad and I didn't like being a sad drunk."

"What did you think of Axel?"

Scooter snorted. "Axel owned a couple of bars and I wasn't a patron."

"Was there a special reason?"

"Most places get to know you and they'll let you have a little credit to carry you over until payday. They'll pass you a free beer now and again. Well, at Axel's places, it was cash on the barrelhead, no credit, and there wasn't a free kernel of popcorn, much less a free Grain Belt beer. It didn't make me want to hang around."

Both Scooter and Elton were nearly helpless without their scooters and rarely took more than a few steps to get from their scooters to chairs. I mentally scratched them from the list of possible suspects.

Chapter 6

I don't really live outside of town, but the housing thins quickly as you get a few blocks from the downtown stoplights. I looped past the row of Norway pines lining Highway 61 along the Two Harbors Golf Course and Curling Club. I don't believe that combination of sports are housed in one facility anywhere outside of Two Harbors, but considering the mix of seasons, the curling rink makes sense. In my view, both sports are an excuse for drinking. I've seen golfers putting while huge May snowflakes swirl around them and drinking beer with chattering teeth. I like hanging out with the curling crews, who prefer drinking Scotch in a warm bar.

I drove to Segog, the little development where I lived, and was surprised to see an orange Lake County dump truck parked near my house where two workers, dressed in their OSHA required lime green, orange, and reflective white vests, held a signpost. Dolores, my elderly neighbor, was leaning on her cane, obviously giving the county guys a piece of her mind. I was tempted to drive past and duck into my garage, pretending to ignore the situation, but I'd been an Eagle Scout and I had the ongoing curse of need-ing to do a daily good deed. I eased behind the truck and saw a look of desperation from the county workers.

"What's up?" I asked as I approached the threesome. Dolores was dressed in a flowered housedress and ortho-pedic shoes. Her hair had been a variety of colors over the years, and the current odd shade of lilac matched the flow-ers in her housedress.

"Peter! I'm so glad you're here," she said, disengaging herself from the two county workers. "You have to explain to these stubborn men that they can't set up a deer cross-ing here. You know that the deer are already wiping out my hostas. Having a deer crossing here would just make the situation unbearable."

I looked at the man with LARRY embroidered on his vest and he pulled out a deer crossing sign from the back of the truck. "I tried to explain that the deer already cross here; we're just putting up a sign to warn drivers."

The other guy, MIKE, according to his vest, was leaning on the new signpost. "We just want to put up the sign and go home for supper. They don't pay us enough to put up with crap like this." He kicked at a steel post driver that was lying at his feet.

Dolores spun like a dervish and gave Mike a glare that could have melted the post driver. "I don't much appre-ciate cuss words." She punctuated her comments by wag-ging her cane ominously. Mike was turning red and Larry was in full grimace. I could see the situation degenerating quickly, mostly because Dolores was about to assault two county workers.

"Larry, does the sign have to go right here?" I asked.

"The county engineer consulted with the department of natural resources and they put this orange spot where the sign is supposed to go." Larry poked his toe at a small spot of orange spray paint on the grass.

"What happens to the orange paint when you drive the post?" I asked.

Mike shrugged. "I guess it kinda goes away. So what?"

"I live in the next house, just across Mrs. Karvonen's driveway, and I would really like to have the deer cross in my yard."

Larry and Mike looked at each other. Mike shrugged. He started scuffing at the orange spot. "Anyplace special you'd like them to cross?" Larry asked.

I turned to Dolores and asked, "Wouldn't it be nice if they crossed by that maple tree?"

She took a couple steps to the side and made a visual survey of the boulevard in front of my house. "I think that the deer would really enjoy crossing there. That tree turns such pretty shades of red, orange, and yellow in the fall. I'm sure they'd love it."

I nodded to Larry and steered Mrs. Karvonen to her front steps. Like all the houses on our street, the style was cookie-cutter bungalow, built by the railroads during the Iron Range boom. We made it up the three concrete steps and through the creaking storm door. Her small porch had a pair of white painted wicker chairs flanking a matching table. Given the regular winds that blow off Lake Superior, there weren't a lot of opportunities to sip iced tea on the porch, but this grouping was ready for service on the rare eighty-degree days we have each summer.

"Dolores, I think you were kind of tough on those nice county workers." In the background I could hear the "clang" of the post driver. "They're nice guys who are just trying to do their jobs."

"Oh, Peter, you are so naïve. I learned a long time ago that if you don't look out for your own interests, people will roll right over you. I learned that lesson from my husband, and that policy has served me well."

By the time I got back to my car the sign project was complete and the guys were pulling away. Larry waved. Mike just shook his head.

Chapter 7

Tuesday

Tuesday morning broke colder but clear. I stepped onto the front step to pick up the newspaper and saw that the Honda's windshield was covered with a thick layer of frost. I made a mental note to leave ten minutes early because I'd have to scrape.

I poured myself a bowl of Rice Krispies and was retrieving the milk when I remembered that it hadn't passed the smell test two days before. My reluctance to go with the milk was reinforced when I poured it down the sink and noted the lumps. Plan B was a move to instant oatmeal. The variety pack had been cleared of all my favorites which left me with the peaches and cream with the little orange bits that tended to be either as chewy as wood chips or as slimy as leeches. As the water heated in the microwave I noted that Axel's murder earned the front page headline of the *Lake County News Chronicle.* The article said that it was the first murder in Two Harbors since the 1940s, and declined to name the victim pending notification of the next of kin.

I looked at the other news headlines and saw that the Great Lakes inaugural cruise-ship season had been interrupted by an outbreak of the extremely contagious Norwalk virus among the passengers. I had a mental image of dozens of people confined to their tiny staterooms with cramps and other stomach disorders that I didn't want to dwell upon. The *Great Lakes Queen* was docked in Thunder Bay, Ontario, where the ship was being decontaminated, and where several of the passengers were hospitalized. The final paragraph riveted my attention when it mentioned that the ship had docked in Duluth on Sunday, and city health officials had notified the local clinics and emergency rooms to watch for cases to show up after the 5-8 day incubation period.

Norwalk virus is miserable in healthy people, but is often deadly in people with poor health and senior citizens. "God, I hope that doesn't make its way to Two Harbors," I thought, making a mental note to mention the article to Jenny. Stomach illnesses tend to go through senior residences like wildfires through a dry pine forest. I had an unsettling thought about Stella Ahonen's birthday party, recalling the Finnish visitors who'd come to Duluth on the cruise ship.

The beeper on the microwave snapped me back to my breakfast tasks and preparations for work.

The BCA's Winnebago was gone from the parking lot, making me hopeful that life might be returning to near normal. I picked up the newspapers from the front sidewalk as I walked in. The *Duluth News Tribune* and the *St. Paul Pioneer Press* both splashed headlines about the murder in a Two Harbors assisted living center.

I drafted April's activities calendar and slipped a copy of it into the director's mail slot for approval. Most of it was repetitive: daily current events discussions, Sunday chapel services (Catholic at 10 and Lutheran at 11) and afternoon popcorn and movies, Tuesday trip to Shopko, Wednesday Bingo, Thursday afternoon trip to Betty's Pies, and Saturday evening card games in the activity room. I penciled in a sing-along for two Fridays, and a book club reading for the other two. Mondays were my day off, and I left them all open. I put a Post-it note on my desk with a reminder to call Duluth about a harbor tour package on the *Vista Queen* later in the summer.

The residents were starting to migrate into the dining room for breakfast as I ducked into the kitchen for a cup of coffee and to check on the latest rumors making their way through the halls. Miriam Millam almost knocked me down as she erupted through the kitchen doors carrying a platter of French toast.

"Dang it, Pete," she uttered as she tried to keep all the food on the platter. "You are going in the OUT door. Use the IN door to go in and the OUT door to go out." She quickly composed herself and presented the platter to the first table with a smile. Miriam was a sturdy farm woman who almost always had a smile. She and her husband owned a dairy farm where she worked eight-hour days milking cows and tending to the calves, bracketing an eight-hour day in Whistling Pines' kitchen. I was amazed by her energy, and her compassion. If anyone was sick or having a tough time, Miriam had a get-well card for us to sign, and she was the one who showed up at their doorstep with a hamburger/noodle hot dish, the Minnesota version of a casserole.

The washing crew was scrubbing and clattering pots and pans as I drew a mug of coffee from the urn. I watched the rhythm of the workers as pancake batter and eggs turned into meals going out the door, followed by the pots moving back to the stainless steel sinks and dishwashers. I took a Honeycrisp apple from a bowl and bit into the tart fruit with a snap. I wasn't part of the flow and the workers ignored me as if I were wallpaper as long as I stayed out of the way.

Two high-school-aged girls flew into the kitchen, through the IN door, and were tittering about someone's date the previous night. Miriam followed behind with an empty platter that she set on the edge of the sink.

"I hear they found a stash of hundred dollar bills in Axel's room," Miriam said as she drew a cup of coffee. She took a sip and stared at me over the rim, waiting for a response.

"I hadn't heard that."

"But the police chief deputized you as an investigator," she said with a sly smile. "I'd think that you'd be the first person to know something like that."

"Yup. You'd think that someone who was an investigator would know that. I guess that must mean I'm not a deputy investigator."

"Either that, or there wasn't any money," she said.

"Or, I can't reveal information to snoops about an ongoing investigation."

"Touché," she said, raising her cup in a mock toast.

"Is that the only rumor this morning?" I asked. "Yesterday there were comments about Axel sleeping around before an appropriate grieving period had passed."

"I heard that they're having bagpipes at the funeral."

"Bagpipes?" I asked, stopping my coffee cup halfway to my mouth. "Axel was Swedish."

"Hey!" she said defensively, "You asked what rumors I'd heard, and that's what I've heard." She paused and gave me the evil eye. "If you're not investigating, why are you so interested in the rumors?"

"I just want to know what's going around. It's easier to keep a lid on things if I can head off the rumors before they get out of hand."

"Rumors have a life of their own," Miriam said with a snort. "There's no way to head them off. The pity is that things sometimes become what people think they are and no amount of fact or truth can turn back the tide. They're a bunch of people with too much time on their hands and too much time alone. They keep mulling things over, and without a sounding board they start to believe something that's not really reasonable."

"Hazel Perkins said that Axel was in a romantic relationship with someone. Have you heard anything about the object of his affection?" I asked.

Miriam stiffened visibly. "I can't imagine a woman having one second for Axel."

"Your body language is saying a lot. I take it that you had a negative experience with him."

"He liked to rub up against the female staff and he got a little handy at times."

"Handy?"

"Peter, how naïve are you?" she asked, shaking her head. "He'd steady himself with a hand on my lower back, and then it would slide down. I'd be serving a table behind him and he'd push his chair back and I'd feel a hand on my thigh. Do you remember when he wore the elastic brace on his wrist for a couple weeks?"

"That was about two years ago, just after I started at Whistling Pines," I said.

"I pulled his hand off my butt in a way that discouraged him from doing it again."

"I assume that you're not the only one that Axel liked."

"Axel liked all the girls, and he liked to tell us about all the money he had, like that would make us look at him as anything but a dirty old man."

"Hey, do you need a dog on the farm?"

"No farmer needs another dog," she replied, eyeing me suspiciously. "Why do you ask?"

"I was just thinking that Tucker needs a home."

Miriam took a deep breath and then let out a sigh. "We don't need another dog, but Tucker's a nice dog. Don't have him put down or anything, but don't put me at the top of the list of possible new owners."

Chapter 8

Toivo "Snuffy" Saari shuffled into the dining room and chose an empty table. He always wore flannel shirts and khaki pants, and the right rear pocket of every pair of pants was nearly worn through by the can of Copenhagen chewing tobacco carried there. He had snow white hair and a scraggly beard stained yellow and speckled with little bits of tobacco. His gums were nearly black from years of tobacco use. I drew a cup of coffee from the urn and carried it to him with a stainless steel pitcher of half-and-half.

"Thanks, Peter," he said in his deep Finnish accent as he poured enough cream in his cup to raise the cholesterol of the entire town of Two Harbors. I was amazed at how slender he was considering the cream, butter, and whole milk he consumed at every meal. He often came to the dining room late, when most of the residents had already eaten. Most times he chose a table where he could be alone. When I sat down, he grimaced.

"May I join you?"

"Looks like you already have," he replied, slurping down some coffee and then staring into his cup.

"Did you hear that Axel died?"

"Yup." He drank some more coffee, and pulled a blue bandana from his pocket, making a show of shaking it open before blowing his nose with a sound that resembled a goose honking. He carefully folded the bandana and put it back in his pocket before returning to his coffee. The silence dragged on for what seemed like a full minute as Snuffy drank coffee and I watched.

"It doesn't seem like many people liked him," I said, trying to leave an opening for expanded conversation.

"Nope."

"Tell me about your experiences with Axel."

Snuffy squirmed in his chair. "Weren't any," he replied, taking a sip of coffee.

"You must've crossed paths with him somewhere, didn't you?" I asked.

Snuffy took a large gulp of coffee, then stood up.

"Are you leaving so soon?" I asked.

"My show's on," he replied, shuffling away from the table.

I watched Snuffy walk away and pitied him for his lonely existence. He had chosen to be so isolated from the rest of the residents that he probably had never been crossed by Axel.

Wendy Plauda was sitting at the next table, working on her daily attempt at the *New York Times* crossword puzzle. Behind her, two of the residents were in the middle of a cribbage game and beyond them, Jingle, the maintenance man, was changing a fluorescent light. Wendy was officially the assistant director, and acted as the liaison between the residents and anyone on the outside, from Medicare to county assistance and funeral homes. In addition to those responsibilities, she sang in a duet with me when we put on music, filled in during the director's vacation, repaired and debugged our computer network, and even helped the aides when they were in a crunch. She had a round face with a Cheshire cat grin that made me think she was about to cause trouble. When Toivo left, Wendy motioned for me to join her.

"Snuffy's a man of few words," she said. "Have you ever noticed his gums? They're so black they remind me of a buzzard's mouth."

"Does he have any friends?'

Wendy tapped her pencil on the puzzle a couple of times. "Most times he avoids people. He'll sit on the fringes of a group, but if anyone tries to engage him, he leaves. I think he spends most of his time in his room watching television, or polishing his old car."

"That seems like a lonely existence," I mused.

"I suppose he's always been really quiet. He never married, and if you're not social, you don't accumulate friends either."

"Garrison Keillor was talking about Norwegian bachelor farmers on *A Prairie Home Companion* and he said, 'Odds are good that the goods are odd.'"

Wendy nodded. She looked down at her crossword and said, "I need an eight-letter word for cross that might end in 'X.'"

"Crucifix," I replied.

Wendy slapped her forehead and said, "Duh."

Jingle was a wiry man, always dressed in blue work clothes, and always on a mission. I walked over as he was moving his ladder to the next light fixture and watched as he expertly replace the burned-out fluorescent bulbs.

"What's up, Pete?" He asked as he moved the ladder to another fixture.

"What do you know about Axel Olson?"

"Um, other than knowing that he's dead, you mean?"

"What kind of guy was he?" I asked.

Jingle pushed back his Minnesota Twins cap and scratched at his thinning blonde hair. It struck me that he was probably old enough to be a resident. "Well, he had me do stuff for him. I don't know more than that."

"Was he nice or grateful for what you did?"

Jingle shrugged. "I don't know about that. He never said thanks or anything, but most people don't. Lots of them have me come to do things just so they have someone to talk with."

"Was he ever mean to you?"

Jingle's eyes sparkled. "No one is ever mean to me." He picked up the ladder and moved it to a new light fixture. "You see, if they're mean to me, nothing gets fixed. People catch onto that quickly."

"And Axel was no fool," I thought to myself.

Chapter 9

Len Rentz was standing at the reception desk checking out all the names on Sunday's visitors' list, starting with the earliest visitor that day. He dragged the list back to my office, first grilling me on the connections and then calling the outliers to ascribe them to a resident. He asked them if they'd seen or heard anything unusual during their visit. Most all of the visitors were local, with a few from as far away as Hinckley, about 75 miles to the south.

Len leaned back from the list. "There were twenty-nine people who signed the visitors' book between 11:45 and 12:30, and they all attended Stella Ahonen's birthday party. I hit seven names that didn't have local phone numbers and all had very Finnish names. Here's my neighbor, Janet. Maybe she can fill in the blanks."

Len dialed his cell phone. "Janet, this is Len Rentz. I'm following up with all the Whistling Pines visitors from the day of Axel Olson's death. I see your name on the visitors' log." He pressed the speakerphone button.

"Hi, Len, I was there for Grandma's birthday party. I guess I hadn't connected the dots between the party and the murder. What's up?"

"I was wondering where you were in the building, and if you'd seen or heard anything unexpected."

"Well the party was in the dining room, and I didn't go anywhere except there." She paused, then laughed. "The only unusual thing I saw was my Aunt Hedvig open her blouse to show everyone her prosthetic breast. She invited everyone to see how natural it felt."

"Um, I was thinking more in the line of criminally strange things."

"Nope, I didn't see anything like that. I just remember all the little old ladies lined up to squeeze Aunt Hedie's fake boob."

Len rolled his eyes and I stifled a laugh. "Geez, Janet, now I've got that in my head too. You really didn't need to share that," he said with a chuckle. "Let me try a different question on you. I've got seven very Finnish names on the visitors' log, but none of them are local. Any chance they were at the birthday party, too, and that you might be able to get me their phone numbers or addresses?" Len read the names from the list.

"They would probably be Aunt Stella's Finnish cousins. They went back to the cruise ship in Duluth as soon as the party was over, and I don't know how you'd contact them. Uncle Arvid Lahti probably has addresses and phone numbers for them once they get back to Finland. But, I think they're supposed to be on the ship another few days before they fly back home. I can probably get you the names and phone numbers of the people that I remember at the party."

"That'd be helpful. I'm not sure that everyone signed in, and I'd like to talk to anyone who was in the building."

Janet rattled off the names she remembered, and Len picked up four people who hadn't signed the log. "I appreciate the help," he offered after scribbling down the names and addresses, then cross-referencing them with the list.

"Say, Len, can I suggest something?"

"Sure."

"I think you should get one of those police belts that have a strap that goes over your shoulder. You really don't have enough hips to hold up that belt of yours, and I saw one with the strap on Barney Fife last night and it seemed to be working for him."

"Thanks, Janet. I have a snap ring sewed onto my belly button that attaches to the buckle, so I don't have problems with it falling down."

"Cool! Did you have that done at the mall in Duluth where they pierce ears?"

"I'm kidding. Thanks for the help."

Jenny's head ducked in my door. "What are you doing here?" she asked me after registering surprise at Len's presence. "It's your day off."

"The ghosts woke me up this morning and told me I had to find Axel's murderer."

Jenny shook her head. "You get two days a week off and you decide to use them chasing murderers? You need to get a life." With that, she was gone.

Len was smirking and shaking his head.

"It's all your fault," I said to him. "I was perfectly happy to go home and be lazy, but you wanted someone on the inside."

"Do like I do," he said. "Put in for comp time to make up for the hours you work on a day off."

"Len, there is no comp time in my job description. If I'm stupid enough to be here on my day off, it's my own fault and Kathy isn't going to give me other time off."

"I have the same problem with the city council," Len said, reaching for the phone. "But it sounds like a good idea when I tell people about it."

Len was about to hang up after the eighth ring when Arvid Lahti answered the phone with a sleepy voice. "Arvid, this is Len Rentz. I was hoping that you could help me out a little with some addresses."

"Who is this?" Arvid yelled. "Hang on a second while I put in my hearing aid."

There was a long pause, followed by an electronic shriek that sounded like microphone feedback. "Okay, now who did you say you were?"

"Len Rentz, from the police department."

"Oh. Hi, Len. What can I do for you?"

"I spoke with your niece, Janet Peterson, and she said that you might be able to help with addresses and phone numbers for the Finnish visitors at Stella's birthday party."

"Janet's a nice girl," Arvid said with a chuckle. "Works pretty hard for herself. I treat her just like my full-blooded Finn relatives even though her dad was a Swede. You really wouldn't know that she was from a mixed marriage like that, would you?"

"Most people don't consider a Finn marrying a Swede a mixed marriage, Arvid."

"Well, you know what they say about Swedes, don't you? You can tell a Swede, but you can't tell him much." Arvid laughed at his joke.

"The Swedes and Norwegians say the same thing about the Finns."

"Well, they got no count saying anything like that. They're just jealous that we're right so much of the time."

"Arvid, can we get back to my original question? I'd like addresses and phone numbers for the Finnish visitors at Stella's party and Janet said you might have them. Is that true?'

"They weren't going back to Finland directly, you know. They were on that tour boat that was going up to Tunder Bay and then to Marquette, Michigan." Arvid pronounced Thunder Bay with a silent H. "I seen on the television that a whole bunch of them tour folks were sick with the shits and got off to go to the hospital."

"Well, I'd like to get numbers for them. I'll try to phone them in a week or two if I still need to."

"You're not thinking that those folks had anything to do with that guy who died at the nursing home, are you? They're all in their eighties and had to have a couple of their kids along to help with the walkers and such."

"They're probably not suspects, but they might've seen or heard something."

"Hah! They all got cataracts and hearing aids. They'd be lucky to be able to hear the dinner bell. I tell you, Len, I think you'd be better looking for somebody a little younger."

"What time did you get to the party, Arvid?"

"Well, I don't surely know. It was before the food got put out, so I suppose that it was a smidge before noon or so. I was about the third one in line, so I got a full portion of all the hot dishes before they got picked over. I can't say I cared much for their rye bread. I guess it was okay for store-bought stuff, but it weren't nothin' compared to when Stella made her Limpa rye. Now that was some good bread. I can picture her walking around the table with that big flat loaf tucked under her arm, carving off hunks as she passed around the table. She was some fine cook."

Len listened patiently and waited for a break in the monologue. "But did you see anything strange that day, or maybe someone who looked out of place?"

"Well there was something that struck me as odd. They made the rice hot dish with beef instead of venison. It just doesn't taste right with beef. I suppose I can understand if they had a bad hunting season, but for a special occasion to be serving beef is pretty odd."

Len grimaced and rolled his eyes, again waiting for a break. "Did you know Axel Olson?"

"Oh, ya. Everyone knew Axel. He was an A number one ass, if you'll excuse my French."

"What made you feel so bad about him?"

"He thought he was a big man and he was always trying to show somebody up. I remember back in the 60s, when I was cutting wood for the pulp mill and trying to raise a family. He had this big tract of pulp wood down by Carlton. It was getting old and starting to die out, like it does right before the birch trees start taking over. Well, I offered him top dollar for the stumpage, but he must've thought he could get more. He wouldn't let me cut there. He never let anyone cut, just let it all die and fall down."

"Did you ask him why he didn't let anyone cut there?"

"Oh, he said that he didn't want me breaking up the roots of the birch trees that were coming in. But it seemed that he just took some sort of strange joy in knowing that I was in a pinch, and that he could make it a little harder for me. He made some sort of comment about Jack-Pine Finns who should figure out how to get a real job. Like I said, he was an A number one ass."

Len interrupted, saying, "Axel had a few pieces of land around the area. Do you know how Axel made the money to buy the land he had?"

"I'm not sure about that. It's not like he ever farmed or logged any of it. I guess I'd assumed that he inherited some money somewhere because it sure didn't seem like he ever worked very hard at the bar business. Mostly I remember him sitting around the VFW and Moose Lodge telling people how much money he had."

"Was he a good family man?"

"Like I said, he was an ass," Arvid said with a snort. "He treated his wife, Enid, and the kids like he owned them. He always had a nice car and nice clothes, and his kids and wife walked around town with clothes that had patches on the patches. I don't know why she stuck with him all those years except that was the way some men were back then. A lot of wives didn't have much say. Not like today.

"Say, Len, I just found the list I had of the Finnish addresses and such. I'm coming into town for a bite of lunch and I could stop by the police station. I suppose you might have a copier there so you could make a copy and leave me with the original?"

"Thanks. Stop by city hall and talk to Shelby. I'll go over right now and tell her that you're coming by in a bit."

Len shut down the speakerphone and shook his head. "The Finnish connection is probably a dead end, but you have to track down every thread."

"Len, if you're trying to convince me to be a cop, you're not making it sound very appealing."

"It's not all running around town with sirens and red lights," Len said.

"Well, I suppose there's the coffee and doughnuts..."

Chapter 10

"Oh, Peter, could you come over here for a minute?" Edith McAllen was gliding down the hall with her new rolling walker that featured a built-in seat. A non-profit group, funded by a mining trust, ran Whistling Pines. They subsidized rent and provided walkers and wheelchairs for the needier residents. Edith followed the birch handrail as she tottered her way toward me. Because of artificial knees and poor equilibrium, she could've been easily mistaken for a drunk.

"What can I do for you, Edith?"

"Well," she started somewhat breathlessly. She was wearing a red knitted sweater and well-worn purple polyester slacks. "I'm a little concerned about this thing with Axel. I've been keeping my door locked, and before I go to bed I put a little stack of aluminum cans against the door so they'll fall over and wake me if someone breaks in and tries to kill me. But I was thinking about calling my son and asking him to bring over a deer rifle that I could keep by my bed."

Swirling visions of little old ladies carrying deer rifles to the dining room passed through my head. My next thought was that we might have to buy bullet-proof vests for the staff. My third thought was to check the resident's handbook to make sure there was a clause forbidding firearms in the building. There was a sign next to the front door that said guns were prohibited on the premises, but the residents might think that's only for visitors. My mind was racing with ugly possibilities.

"Now, Edith, no one's going to break into your apartment and do you harm. You don't need a gun, and I don't think that we allow the residents to have guns in their rooms anyway."

"I've got a right to protect myself, and it sure seems that if Axel had had a gun he'd still be alive. He was a war hero, you know. He probably would've shot that guy who shot him. Instead, the killer is still roaming the halls, probably looking for his next victim."

"Axel wasn't shot, Edith. And, I'm pretty sure that the person who killed Axel wasn't a resident."

Edith gave me the "evil eye" with one lid partially closed. She drew in a deep breath and was ready to say something when Howard Johnson came around the corner.

"Hello, Edith," he said.

He nodded to me as he passed. He moved smoothly, his white-haired head held high. Even his shoes had a luster that made me believe they'd seen a shining cloth that morning.

In an effort to change the topic I threw out the first thing that came to mind. "I've got a sign-up list for people who want to ride the shuttle to Axel Olson's funeral."

Howard stopped and looked over his shoulder at me. "I doubt that you'll need the big van. I suspect you'll have a hard time filling a Volkswagen Beetle if you limit it to people who would claim Axel as their friend." His pace quickened as he left.

"Are you going to the funeral, Edith?" I asked, thinking back to Howard's earlier comments.

"I haven't decided yet. I might go just to hear the bagpipes."

"Where did you hear that there are going to be bagpipes?"

"It was all the talk at lunch. I guess they had to go all the way to Thunder Bay to find a decent piper who knew how to play 'Amazing Grace.'"

"Wendy and I are in charge of the funeral music, and we don't have any plans for bagpipes," I explained.

"Yup, I heard that you and Wendy were trying to squash the bagpipe idea, but I guess the family is making all the arrangements in spite of you."

"I'll tell you what. I'm going to call Axel's son right now to see if he knows anything about bagpipes."

"I guess you'd better, Pete, 'cause you'll sure look silly trying to sing some hymn when the bagpipes come marching in playing 'The Charge of the Light Brigade.'"

"'The Charge of the Light Brigade' is a poem, not a song. 'Half a league, half a league, half a league onward. All in the Valley of Death, Rode the six hundred.'"

Edith frowned and then tottered away humming "The Battle Hymn of The Republic," which I suppose could be confused with "The Charge of the Light Brigade" if your memory is a little off-kilter.

After my discussion with Edith, I searched out Wendy to see what she'd been planning for funeral music. I found her sitting at a dining table with a corner of the linen tablecloth peeled back, and the bud vase pushed aside. She was concentrating on a crossword puzzle and sipping a glass of Mountain Dew. The other fifteen tables were neatly set up for the next meal, a red or white carnation on each table. Wendy was backlit by the large windows that gave peeks of Lake Superior across the expansive lawn. The grass was still brown, waiting for a few warm days of sunshine. A dozen hundred-year-old white pines swayed as the lake winds ripped through their branches. The architect who designed Whistling Pines had been standing under those trees, surveying the property when a wind came up, creating a whistle through the pines and providing him with the name Whistling Pines.

"Edith McAllen cornered me and we got into a discussion about Axel's funeral music," I said as I slid a chair back from the table and sat down. "She's convinced that we're going to have bagpipes."

"Did you know that Edith's nickname was Busty?" Wendy asked, not looking up from her puzzle.

"Who told you that?" I asked, trying to picture a younger version of Edith with an expansive bosom.

"Edith did, when I was helping her fill out medical assistance forms. Now she says that it's a race to see whether it's the right one or the left one that gets to her knees first." Wendy gave me her Cheshire cat smile, knowing it would take hours to banish that image from my mind.

I heard chuckling from behind me and turned to find Miriam drawing a cup of coffee from the urn. "One of our old cows has teats that almost drag on the ground when she's out grazing."

"Can we move this discussion in another direction?" I asked.

Miriam frowned. "I thought you were the one who started the conversation about Busty McAllen."

The door to the patio opened and Becky, one of the high school girls who worked part-time in the kitchen, came inside, Tucker leading the way. Tucker was straining at the leash and nearly dragging her. The contest was still undecided until Tucker stepped on one of his own ears and did a slow somersault. "I'm getting so tired of taking Tucker out to pee on the bushes. Can't we find someone who will take him home?" Becky asked.

Miriam looked as if she'd suddenly forgotten something in the kitchen and Wendy's puzzle was suddenly more interesting.

"What's a five-letter word for pismire?" Wendy waggled a #2 pencil between the fingers of her right hand. There were teeth marks all over the yellow paint.

"What?"

"I need a five-letter word for pismire," she said, pointing to a spot near the bottom of the puzzle. "It's here in the puzzle, and it looks like the second and third letters are 'M.'" She turned the puzzle so I could see the open boxes around the two M's. "See, it says pismire," she said pointing to the clue with the tip of her pencil.

"I have no idea what pismire is, and we really need to talk about bagpipes," I said in exasperation.

Wendy cocked her head and stared at the clues, totally ignoring the bagpipe issue. "If you know a famous sportswriter whose name starts with COS, I could get the first letter of pismire."

"Howard Cosell is the only sportswriter I know of whose name starts with COS."

"C-O-S-E-L-L. That would mean that pismire starts with an EMM and two blanks. What's the rest?"

"Wendy, listen to me," I said, grabbing the pencil from her hand. "We have to talk about funeral music. It seems that everyone thinks that we're going to have bagpipes and I don't know a thing about it."

"Geez, don't get your undies in a bunch just because you don't know the word for pismire," she said, snatching the pencil back. "I thought you went to college to get a huge vocabulary so you'd know how to use words like pismire to impress people."

"Bagpipes! Talk to me about bagpipes!"

"I don't know where you found them, but the residents are pretty much pumped about the idea of bagpipes at the funeral." She continued to study the puzzle. "If a typical shower present is a *layette*, and that fits all the other ways, then the last letter in pismire is a T."

"I haven't got bagpipes. I don't plan to get bagpipes, and I'd like to know who started the rumor that there's going to be bagpipes at the funeral."

"I've got it! With Maeve as Prince Arn's wife, that makes 'emmet' the answer to pismire. That seems kind of stupid. I wonder if pismire is somebody's last name?"

I snatched the puzzle and pencil from Wendy's hands and held them behind my back. "Tell me if you've arranged for bagpipes for the funeral."

"I thought you were taking care of the pipers," she said with a shocked look on her face. "I've got an opening hymn and a vocal solo, but I thought that since you were lining up bagpipes that they'd be best for the recessional. I know they only have nine notes, so that really limits the songs they can play, but I've heard 'Amazing Grace' on the pipes and they give it a real mournful edge that befits a funeral."

I closed my eyes. "There are no bagpipes."

"There are going to be a lot of disappointed old ladies who are looking forward to hearing bagpipes at the funeral," she said, stealing the pencil back and jabbing it in the air for emphasis. "If you couldn't find a piper, why did you tell all the people that there are going to be bagpipes?"

"That's what I'm trying to tell you, Wendy. I didn't tell anyone that we were having bagpipes. I have no idea where the rumor came from." I handed the crossword puzzle back to her. "I thought maybe it was something that you or the family had arranged."

"Not me," she replied, sliding the crossword back onto the table. "Hey, do you know a four-letter word for the Hawaiian state bird that starts with N? The second letter might be an E."

"Plan for something other than bagpipes for the recessional," I said, pushing myself back from the table. "Focus on something that can be played on the organ."

"It might be Nene, but that hardly seems like the name for a bird." She looked up with a twinkle in her eye. "Tell you what. I'll check with the organist to see if she can set the organ to sound like bagpipes, and I can play "Amazing Grace" for the recessional. No, how about 'Loch Lomond?' You know the song, 'You take the high road and I'll take the low road.'"

I threw up my hands. "Whatever!"

My mind was on the nonexistent bagpipes when I stepped out of the dining room and into Len Rentz. He managed to put his hand on my chest in an effort to avert being bowled over by my mad rush.

"Easy, Peter."

"Oh! I'm sorry," I said, catching his arm in time to stop his spin. "I'm a little stressed out over bagpipes."

"I heard something about bagpipes," Len said as he reestablished his footing. "It seemed a little strange for a Swedish funeral."

"Come with me," I said, waving Len into the director's office. I closed the door.

"I'm not sure where that rumor started, but there are no bagpipes."

"It's funny how rumors grow by leaps and bounds when you get a bunch of people in a closed community. We have the same problem in the city offices."

"I don't imagine you came here to talk about rumors."

"Let's go up to Axel's apartment and look around again," Len said, reaching for the door.

"Um, the room is sealed," I said as Len walked to the elevator.

"The people from the state are through. They released the scene," Len said, pushing the elevator button. "We won't be disturbing any evidence."

The elevator doors opened and Maude Thibeault hesitated for a second when she saw Len's uniform. She looked up at his face and smiled. "Lenny, how are you?" She stepped out far enough to block the doors, and put her hand on Len's arm. "You weren't the brightest boy in third grade, but people say that you're a pretty good policeman."

"Thanks for the encouragement, Mrs. Thibeault," pronouncing it Tee-bow. "I try to make up for my shortcomings by being thorough and diligent."

She patted Len's arm and stepped past him. "That's probably the most you can expect, you coming from a German family and all."

I looked for an explanation, but Len nudged me toward the open elevator. When the door closed he smiled. "Mrs. Thibeault was a young woman whose parents were killed in France during the German occupation. She didn't have much time for Germans, and since my parents were the only family in Two Harbors with a German name, we caught a lot of her wrath, in and out of school."

The elevator door opened and we stepped into an empty hallway. "My father and grandfather both proudly served in the U.S. Army. But, Mrs. Thibeault was more interested in her festering German hatred than in facts."

We stopped in front of Axel's door and Len pulled away the yellow crime scene tape. "But it's not just her. My father fought the Japanese in the Pacific and saw some things that he won't talk about to this day. My brother was looking at a new Toyota Camry a couple of years ago and my dad told him that no son of his would ever own a Jap car."

I pulled out my ring of keys and unlocked Axel's door with the master key. "So, did your brother buy the Toyota?"

"Nope, and we never talked about it again."

I stepped aside and let Len take the lead. We stopped at the edge of the living room, looking at the blood-stained carpet where I'd found Axel. "What are we looking for?" I asked.

The room was untouched since the crime scene techs had gone through, leaving a thin layer of black finger-print dust on all the surfaces. Axel's furniture was neat and clean, but dated. A gold and green plaid couch, which appeared to be a hide-away bed, took up one wall. Hanging over the couch was a large framed print of a seascape. The other wall had matching green recliners set on each side of a small table with a lamp. Axel's sole form of entertain-ment, other than Tucker, was a 19-inch television with a loop antenna on top, leading to a convertor box. I'd heard Axel was too cheap to pay for cable when he could get one Duluth station very nicely with his garage sale antenna and the converter box paid for by the government.

A small desk under the window had pigeonholes, each with a neat stack of envelopes or papers. A ceramic coffee mug, emblazoned with the logo of the local home health care company, held scissors and an assortment of pens and pencils. A lap drawer had been left partially open by the investigators.

Past an open pocket door was a bedroom alcove with a double bed and a bedside table. A dog-eared paperback lay next to the lamp near a pair of reading glasses. The bedding was piled in the center of the bed, in contrast to Axel's usual military neatness.

Notably missing from the apartment were pictures. Nearly every resident decorated their apartment with pictures of their children, grandchildren, and great grandchildren. Some apartments were so cluttered with photos it appeared that the walls required reinforcement to sustain the load. Every desktop and dresser were usually covered with picture frames. The only picture Axel had was of him getting a military medal. It was now on the kitchen counter, its broken glass and frame dusted with black powder.

Len put his hands on his hips and studied the room. "I don't know. Considering that the BCA went over the place with a fine-toothed comb, I don't expect that there's much here that hasn't been examined."

"Did they find anything of interest?"

Len nodded toward the desk. "The desk drawer was ajar and the BCA found a military medal inside."

"Axel really was a hero?" I asked.

"Apparently," Len replied. "The BCA found a British decoration with his name engraved on the back."

"Did the BCA have any other revelations?" I asked.

"No one told the BCA that Axel lived with a dog, so I got a nasty message complaining that it was going to take them a year to sort through the shopping bag of dog hair they got in their vacuum." Len chuckled a little. "They actually asked when the rug had last been vacuumed."

"Housekeeping runs a vacuum through every week, but I doubt that they are as diligent as the crime scene techs."

"Their other question was what breed of dog shed that much."

"Tucker is a basset hound mix," I said. "I think he weighs forty five pounds."

"They thought that the dog had to be the size of a pony to leave that much hair behind."

"Um, Axel claimed that he was part St. Bernard, but I doubt that has much to do with the quantity of hair. I think he's just a prolific shedder," I offered.

"I appreciate a little gallows humor sometimes," Len said. "But let's get serious and look for a murder weapon. The M.E. said that the knife was no more than a half-inch wide and six inches long."

I did the math quickly in my head. "That's somewhere between a filet knife and an ice pick."

Len walked into the kitchen and started pulling out drawers. "I was thinking a stiletto or maybe a sharp letter opener."

I wandered into the bathroom and stared at the white tile, the white tub, the white sink, white towels and the birch cabinets and thought I was going snow blind. There wasn't a smudge, a stray hair, a crumpled tissue, or wrinkled towel in sight. I opened the medicine cabinet and stared at the array of bottles.

"Looking for the little blue pills?" I jumped at the sound of Len's voice. I hadn't heard him come into the bathroom.

"Not specifically," I replied.

"The county deputies told me about the confrontation in the hall. Some little woman accused Axel of being a lothario."

"Actually, she used a different word, but the meaning was clear — she thought that his wife hadn't been dead long enough to be with other women."

"So, is there a bottle of Viagra on the shelf?"

The shortest bottle was Vick's Vaporub, and the tallest was glucosamine. The range of meds ran from aspirirn to zinc lozenges, lined up in alphabetical order. "The only prescription medications in here are Percocet, Lipitor, and Lasix."

I pulled open the drawer under the sink. I started picking up the items and read the labels. "Crest. Preparation H."

"Do you think any of the female staff members might've had something romantic going with him?" Len asked.

"No way. I can't imagine any of them having anything to do with him. They've said that he was a creep who was always trying to cop a feel or peek down the front of their blouses." I put the tubes back in the drawer and used a little toilet paper to wipe the black fingerprint powder off my fingers. "But he claimed to have lots of money, he had a car, and he bathed regularly. That's about as good as it gets when you're an octogenarian."

"Come back to the living room, Pete." We stopped behind Axel's favorite recliner and looked at the blood stain on the floor. "What do you see?"

"I see a large spot of blood on carpeting that will have to be replaced before anyone else can move in here."

"No tipped tables or lamps or other signs of a struggle," Len observed, ignoring my comment. "The coroner didn't find any skin under his fingernails, defensive wounds, or scratches to indicate that he'd been in a struggle."

"So, it was someone he knew?" I asked, trying to figure out if Len was testing me or just letting me engage in the process.

"Or, it was someone who was able to sneak up on him."

"Axel wasn't deaf, but he always had the television volume cranked up pretty loud," I mused. "I guess someone could have come in the door and walked up behind him."

"What about the dog? Wouldn't he make a racket if someone came in the room?"

"Tucker has a happy bark and he kind of bays or howls when he's unhappy. Maybe Axel wouldn't notice if the barking sounded friendly."

"In that case, it would have been someone that Tucker recognized," Len said.

I briefly contemplated the list of residents. "There are only a dozen men, one less now with Axel gone, and I've already spoken with most of them. I suppose I could start talking to each of the women, too."

I tried to sound skeptical, since I really had many other things to do besides chatting up all the female residents. Len gave me a sly smile and I knew this wouldn't be an argument I could win.

"But, Len, they all want to chat, sometimes for hours. It could take days, or even weeks, for me to have a meaningful discussion with each of them."

Len patted me on the shoulder. "Take good notes. I find that without good notes all the interviews start to run together in my head by the time we get to trial."

Chapter 11

All the staff carried cell phones with a voice-activated walkie-talkie feature. Jenny's voice came to me as if she were hooked on my belt. "Peter, could you give us a hand in Peggy Johnson's room, please?"

"Jenny," I said, pausing for the circuit to open in response to my voice. "I'm on my way."

Peggy was a stout woman who'd worked a dairy farm with her husband. They'd sold the farm, but Peggy had plenty of muscle packed on her frame, which had slowly turned to gelatin in her retirement. She lived independently, roaming the halls with her walker, eating bread with lots of real butter and drinking whole milk at every meal. Her apartment door was jammed open and I could hear voices in the bathroom.

Peggy was sitting on the toilet with a towel draped over her lap while Jenny and one of the aides, Marcy Copeland, squatted next to her. Peggy looked up at me as red slowly crept up her neck and into her face. Her blue slacks were around her ankles. As always, her retouched brown hair was carefully permed to make her look taller than her five-foot two-inch frame.

"Oh, Peter. I'm so sorry to drag you up here."

Jenny pulled me to Peggy's side. "I'm going to slip a Posey belt around Peggy's tummy, and when we've got that buckled, I want you to lift on the belt from the back while you gently lift Peggy's arm with your free hand."

Peggy was shaking her head. "This is so embarrassing. To think that I had to drag people up here to get me off the toilet." She clucked her tongue as Jenny and Marcy slipped the heavy cotton belt around her middle.

"It's all because of the Reader's Digest. I got caught up in an article about a family that was raising triplets, and time just slipped away from me. Next thing you know, I'm sitting here and my knees and hips are locked up."

Jenny smiled and nodded, signaling me to start the lift. Marcy stood in front of Peggy, and we eased her into a stooped standing position, still mostly poised over the porcelain. I discreetly stared at the open bathroom door, where Kathy, the director, had appeared during the process.

"OK, now give me a second to get my knees in gear," Peggy said as Marcy raised her slacks. Jenny reached to unbuckle the Posey belt and I got a brief whiff of her perfume as she mouthed "Thank you."

"Peter, when you've got a second, I'd like to talk to you about the funeral," Kathy said as she pushed Peggy's walker within reach. "Someone called about bagpipes."

"I knew it!" Peggy said, surprising us all. "I told them that the bagpipes weren't just a rumor! Wait until I call Audrey."

"Now wait, Peggy," I said. "I'm in charge of the music, and I haven't arranged for bagpipes."

"I know," Peggy replied as she slowly pushed past me. "It's the family. They're doing it because Axel was so proud of his service with the Brits during the war."

Kathy, with her perfectly coifed hair and gray silk blouse, peeked around the door, gave me a withering glare and nodded toward the hallway. In the hall, she jammed a pink message slip at me. "Tell me about the bagpipes, Peter."

"There are no bagpipes," I said as I unfolded the message.

"Then, explain why I got a call from the St. Paul Police Federation. They want to know what time we want the pipers, and if we want a full police honor guard, too." Kathy stood with her arms folded across her chest.

The message was from Angus McTavish and gave a St. Paul, Minnesota, area code.

"I honestly don't know a thing about this," I said, waving the note. "Someone started a rumor that there's going to be bagpipes and it seems to have gotten out of hand."

"I spoke with Mr. McTavish and he said that they'd had a message from a woman asking them to contact Peter, at Whistling Pines, who was asking about the pipers for a retired policeman's funeral. It seems the only hitch is that they can't find Axel Olson on the roster of retired St. Paul policemen."

"I don't think he was a cop. I think he was dabbling in local real estate, and mostly lived to piss people off." I tried to hand the note back to Kathy, who kept her arms crossed.

"Please call Mr. McTavish, who told me to call him Gus, and advise him of the confusion about Axel's status as a police veteran and offer him our apologies."

Kathy had a persona that went from Jeckyl to Hyde in a matter of seconds. I'd seen her charm little old ladies and their families with a delightful smile and a soft voice. The other half of that persona was reserved for the staff, who have all suffered frostbite as the result of Kathy's icy glares, or have looked forward to the brimstone of the depths of hell when she put an edge on her voice and whispered invectives to them. At this point, her voice was so soft that I had to lean closer to hear her words. It was nice that she'd said "please," but there was no confusion that this was nothing less than an order which was not to be questioned. I quickly assessed my options, which seemed to be calling Gus McTavish immediately or starting to clear out my desk.

"I'm on it," I said, expecting some expression of thanks or encouragement. The glare continued, which left me with the belief that I wasn't moving quickly enough toward a phone.

"One other thing, Peter," Kathy caught me in mid-turn.

"Yes?"

"It seems that the residents are very interested in hearing bagpipes at Axel's funeral. Perhaps you should see if you can find a piper."

I turned to leave again, only to be caught short. "Peter, any costs will have to come out of your entertainment budget unless you can get the family to pay."

"I understand."

As I scrambled away I quickly ran through the options to pay for bagpipes out of my budget. I came to the quick conclusion that there weren't any options, short of parking the van for half the year and giving out pennies instead of dimes as Bingo prizes. Those being unreasonable, I came to the conclusion that I had to find a way to get Axel's family to pay.

My office had been a storage closet until the mess in my cubicle, which was visible from the lobby, became such an eyesore that Kathy decided to give up the storage space. She also suggested that the door remain closed at all times.

I paused at the corkboard mounted on my door to see how many of the residents had signed up for a ride to the funeral. I'd left sixteen open slots, which was our van's capacity. All sixteen slots were filled and additional names crammed the open area at the bottom and sides of the sheet. "It looks like we'll be making at least two trips between Whistling Pines and the church," I said to myself. By contrast, the sign-up sheet for the trip to Walmart had only three signatures.

I filed the drafts of activity plans with the confirmations from the businesses that agreed to let a busload of seniors invade. Walmart was always great, but some of the local restaurants were less than enthusiastic about a busload of elderly people who ate slowly, tipped poorly, sometimes got trapped in the bathrooms, and stole the toothpicks and mints near the cash register. After a few minutes of filing I found the phone and had a bare surface to write.

Gus McTavish of the Police Federation Emerald Society sounded like a jovial guy who laughed heartily when I explained the rumor mill run amok and all the little old people badgering me about the bagpipes.

"I wish you luck, Peter. Sounds like you've got a challenge."

"Do you know of any bagpipe groups in northern Minnesota?"

"Well, there used to be some old farts who played up in McGregor, but they weren't a group or anything. I think they used to pull out the pipes on St. Patrick's Day just to irritate their neighbors. I could see if any of our guys can remember their names. I suppose there's a chance they may all be dead. They weren't spring chickens when we heard about them in the '80s."

"Please give me a call if you get a name, but there isn't much time to get this lined up. The funeral is in a few days.

Is there any way I could talk you into sending up a piper or two for the day?"

Gus laughed. "Peter, how far north are you, a hundred and fifty miles from St. Paul? That means a whole day in the car to play 'Amazing Grace' and 'Loch Lomond' for a bunch of little old ladies. I doubt that I'd be able to find anyone who would be interested in taking a day of vacation for that duty."

After offering my understanding and thanks, I hung up and pulled up Google on my computer. The search combination of bagpipes and funeral brought up a whole string of websites for people who play bagpipes for a variety of events. One very clever site, pipes4hire.com, offered the services of a piper for any event in the Chicago area. Another site was specific to Montreal, and there were dozens in Scotland and Ireland offering local piper services. When I narrowed the search to bagpipes and Minnesota I got an interesting string of possible hits that had nothing to do with me finding a piper for a funeral in two days. I did find a massage therapist in Winnipeg, Manitoba, who advertised her services on a web page that showed her holding bagpipes and wearing only a kilt while "O Canada" played in the background. The note at the bottom of her web page suggested that customers would find out whether a piper wore anything under his, or her, kilt and listed a 1-900 phone number, which I knew was a phone exchange that charged by the minute. I had an inkling that this massage therapist had some other sidelines, like a phone sex business, that might not be acceptable to many of my senior citizens. It was at this point in my doldrums that Jenny chose to check-in on me.

"Um, Peter, I don't think we're allowed to view that type of material on the work computers," she said, peeking over my shoulder. "Besides, I can give you a better massage than some bimbo from the Internet."

Embarrassed at being caught with a half-nude woman on my computer screen, I stammered, "I...I found this in my search for bagpipes in the Minnesota region."

"I'd say she should find kilts that match the plaid of her bagpipes," Wendy, who appeared out of nowhere, added, looking over my other shoulder. "Who gave the OK to check out porn on Peter's computer?"

"I wasn't looking at porn," I explained. "I was looking for someone to play bagpipes."

"So, you've got *her* coming for the funeral?" Wendy asked as she reached across my keyboard to page down to the contact information.

"No! I haven't got her coming to the funeral." I quickly clicked the mouse to return to the search screen before we accidentally sent in a query or something. "She's somewhere in Canada and she probably only uses the bagpipes as a prop for her ad."

"I could load a CD on the church sound system," Wendy offered, trying to get back to the screen with the topless piper. "And, we could have her stand up front pretending to play the pipes."

I wrestled the keyboard away from Wendy and unplugged the mouse. "Stop it! We're not having a topless hooker pretend to play bagpipes for Axel's funeral!"

Jenny was trying to stifle a laugh while watching Wendy try to wrest the computer keyboard back from me. "Shh. Be quiet. Here come some residents," said Jenny.

Peggy Johnson wheeled her walker to my door just as Wendy pulled the keyboard out of my hands. "Oh, am I interrupting something?"

"Not at all," I said. "Wendy was just leaving."

"Well, I got in touch with my sister Olivia. She's at a nursing home in Eveleth. She's going to have her activities director call you, Peter, to get the details of the funeral. They might bring a busload of people over to hear the bagpipes, too."

"Peggy, it's not a concert; it's a funeral," I said, trying to hide my irritation. "I don't think it's appropriate to bring people to Axel's funeral who've never met him."

Peggy stuck out her wrinkled lower lip, like a pouting child. "But no one's ever heard bagpipes in person before. It's going to be such a treat."

Behind me, Wendy's fingers were flying over the keyboard. Suddenly, "O Canada" was playing. "Peggy, wouldn't it be fun to have this girl play for the funeral?" Wendy asked.

"Well, she certainly looks like she could play the pipes, but I think she'd be awfully cold, not wearing anything to cover her little boobies." Peggy pressed closer. "I've always wondered if they had underwear under those kilts."

Jenny finally lost it and started to laugh, which she quickly turned into a fake coughing fit. She put her hand under Peggy's arm and guided her to the door. "I think we need to leave Wendy and Peter to their search for a piper."

"Maybe we can get Conrad Carlson to play 'Loch Lomond' on the accordion," Wendy said as she shut the Canadian site down. "Connie was playing at the Dew Drop Inn last weekend and did a pretty good rendition of 'You Picked a Fine Time To Leave Me, Lucille.' He said he'd never tried it before, so it was all by ear, and it would've brought tears to Kenny Rogers' eyes."

I just shook my head. "Yes, Wendy, I think that probably would've brought tears to Kenny Rogers."

Chapter 12

Irene Borzek was exiting the elevator as I passed and hailed me down. I pretended to not hear, fearing another bag-pipe discussion, but she trumpeted my name so every head in the lobby turned to see who was making the commotion.

"Peter," she said breathlessly. "I've been trying to catch you since those policemen talked to me." She was pushing a walker with an oxygen tank strapped to one of the legs. The green hose ran from the tank to the canula under her nose. Her face would've been pasty except for the layers of powder and rouge she put on each morning. Today she'd chosen a darker brown that contrasted with her white hair, making her look like she'd been to a tanning salon.

I spun around and turned her toward a quiet corner of the commons, away from the front desk. "How can I help, Irene?"

We stopped a few feet past the aviary where the doves were cooing, and waited for Irene to catch her breath. She'd been a bookkeeper for the local car dealership until her retirement, so she was a whiz with numbers, and often beat the others handily at bridge because she could remember which cards had been played when short-term memory problems haunted many of the other players.

"Peter," she wheezed, "you know that I live right under Axel's room. Tucker had been baying for a few minutes before I heard the thump that was probably Axel falling down. I heard voices, too, but I couldn't tell what they were saying."

"Was it a male or female voice that you heard?"

"Well, I heard Axel quite clearly. He was laughing about something, but the other voice was too soft to make out, especially with Tucker making all that noise."

"Axel was laughing?" I asked.

"I certainly think so. It sounded like he was laughing and the other voice was soft." I looked at the hearing aid that looped behind her ear, wondering if she was credible.

Peggy Johnson edged over to where we were standing and heard that we were discussing Axel. "Bert Sugarman did it!" She announced in her outdoor voice.

I patted Irene on the arm, then pulled Peggy closer, hoping that the close proximity would make her lower her voice. "Who is Bert Sugarman and why do you think he did it?"

"I saw him at Mass this morning," she said in a slightly softer version of the outdoor voice. I peeked at the reading room. Every head was turned to hear Peggy's pronouncement. "It was his eyes. He had so much evil pent up inside him that his eyes were bugging out. I don't know what else could cause that much evil to push that hard. Well, not unless he's gambling again."

I pressed my fingertips to my temples and closed my eyes. "His eyes bug out, so he's the murderer?"

"It's obvious," Peggy stated emphatically.

"His eyes have stuck out since he was a kid," Irene said. "He's always looked a little like one of those tropical bush babies. That's why all the kids used to call him 'Bug.'"

The always helpful Wendy happened to hear all the conversation and drifted over. "I think he looks more like one of those honey drippers that they sell as pets." The corners of her mouth crinkled with a hint of a grin, and then she left me with the escalating Sugarman discussion.

"No," Peggy stated firmly. "His eyes have gotten much more buggy since Axel's death. His eyes got that way when he hit puberty, 'cause of all those carnal thoughts he kept pent up inside. But now, they're much buggier."

There was a flash of rusty brown at my feet, followed by Miriam, sporting a new, close-cropped haircut and a white uniform. "Tucker, come back here! Bad dog, Tucker!" she yelled as she raced past us. She yelled a saltier version of Tucker's name as she chased the loping dog, who managed to slip out the front door. "You little *ucker, get back here!"

Chapter 13

I was staring at the May schedule, my mind cluttered with the scattered comments about Bert Sugarman's buggy eyes and visions of Miriam racing through the lobby shouting profanities. None of the dots were connecting across any of my discussions with the residents. Added to my discomfort was the ongoing discussion about bagpipes, and my embarrassment over getting caught viewing the phone sex website.

My concentration was broken by the sound of someone clearing her throat. Standing at my door was a woman whose stature must have garnered stares wherever she went.

"Are you Peter?" she asked.

She was well over six feet tall, had hair so big it would be the envy of many country music stars, and was more than full-figured. She was made up to look younger, but the crow's feet around her eyes and the furrowed brow said she was closer to her fiftieth birthday than the fortieth. She wore a loose sweatshirt that failed to hide her expansive bosom. A pair of jeans that appeared to be a size too small highlighted her curves. Her fingernails were long and painted an ungodly shade of pink that matched her lipstick.

"Excuse me," she said, "my eyes are up here." She pointed to her face, which brought me to a full Norwegian blush. This wasn't a warming of the neck, or pinkness of the cheeks. This was the full, fire-engine-red flaming of the face.

"Sorry, I was trying to see..."

"I know what you were trying to see. What I was hoping to see was someone named Peter who is working on arrangements for my father's funeral."

"I'm sorry that we got off to a bad start," I said, pushing myself out of the chair and offering a handshake. "I'm Peter."

She took my hand briefly, with a look that said she thought I'd been picking up after Tucker with bare hands. "Just tell me what's going on with the funeral and I'll get the hell out of here and you can get back to..." She looked at the piles of papers scattered across my desktop. "So you can get back to whatever it is that you can accomplish in this pigsty."

I flashed back to condescending discussions I'd had with Axel and realized that this apple hadn't fallen far from the tree. "Well, we've got the minister and the Lutheran church set up for Friday afternoon at two. Wendy, our assistant director, is going to sing a solo, and we're working on plans for the processional and recessional. Do you have any thoughts about whether the family would prefer traditional or contemporary music?"

Her eyes narrowed. "You didn't mention bagpipes."

"I...um...didn't know that your father liked bagpipes."

"Everyone's been telling me that you've got bagpipes lined up for the funeral."

"Well, I made a couple calls, but I don't think that we'll be able to get a piper lined up on such short notice."

The blonde Amazon crossed her arms across her ample chest. "My father hated bagpipes. I don't know what kind of loony bin you run here," she let that sink in for a second and then added, "but my father's army unit was camped next to a company of Canadians in Korea and he said he got so sick of hearing them marching to the bagpipes that he threatened to burn the pipes when they were out on patrol."

"So, we're clear on the bagpipes," I said. Quickly sorting through a small pile of papers I came up with a list of songs that Wendy and I had developed for a funeral in our chapel the previous month, and I offered them to her. "The top songs are traditional hymns and the lower section is contemporary. What guidance would you offer on behalf of the family?"

"My father was a shit," she said, eyeing the paper like it also had been soiled. "I wouldn't waste a hymn on him. For that matter, you'd better check the foundation of that church because it's likely to crack when you wheel his casket in." She threw the list of songs my direction, turned and stepped out of the office, then hesitated and turned back to me.

"On second thought, get the bagpipes. I'll pay whatever it costs. I'm sure it'll make him turn in his grave. I'd also suggest that you contact the mortician and have him put a stake in Axel's heart, just so he doesn't rise in protest during the service."

"He wanted to be cremated," I said.

"Of course he wanted cremation. It's the cheapest," she said. "I told the funeral director to put him in the most expensive casket he could find and to put it into a lead-lined vault. That ought to put a grimace on his face for eternity." With that, she spun around and disappeared.

Wendy stuck her head in the door. "Who was the blonde lard bowl with an attitude?"

"Axel's daughter," I replied. "I'm not entirely sure why she stopped by. She wanted to know about the funeral arrangements, but really didn't want to give me any input."

"So, what did she say?" Wendy asked.

"I think she wanted to rant about what a stinker her father had been."

Wendy lurched forward into my office, then spun around, looking annoyed.

Maude Thibeault pushed her walker into the cramped office, striking Wendy in the shins. "Was that Christine, Axel's daughter?" she asked loudly.

"Yes," I replied as Wendy rubbed her shin. "Do you know her?"

"Oh no, I only heard Axel telling people that his daughter had a gland problem and that she got really big. That was one big girl that came outta here. She had boobs the size of watermelons."

"Does she live nearby?" I asked, hoping to redirect the conversation.

Maude looked at me as if I were a slow child. "She's the bimbo who runs Axel's bar downtown. My nephew was there when she ran a bunch of Hell's Angels out one night when they got lippy. Sat on one of 'em and almost suffocated him before the cops showed up. I guess it was pretty pathetic seeing this big biker guy with leather and tattoos thanking a cop for saving him."

"What do Axel's other children do?" Wendy asked.

"Well, he's got a son, named Daryl or Darren, who's a diesel mechanic on the Iron Range. He wasn't much of a student, so Axel didn't trust him to do anything responsible, like running the bar. The other son is an accountant who runs Axel's apartments. His name is Donald. He was a really good math student, and I hear that he runs the apartments with an iron fist, just like his father."

"Where does Axel own apartments?" I asked.

"Oh, all over the place. He'd find people who were going bankrupt, or were having some financial problems, and he'd scoop them up for pennies on the dollar. I heard that he bought one from a drug dealer who had to get quick cash to take a trip."

"It sounds like Axel was quite a wheeler and dealer," Wendy commented.

Maude turned her walker to face Wendy. "Axel was an outright bastard who took advantage of people. Compared to Axel, a used car salesman looks like Mother Teresa. He didn't just use people, he relished the victory, and would rub people's noses in it for years."

My mind quickly ran through the new list of people who could be suspects. Len Rentz would have to run through piles of property records to see who Axel might've scammed over the years.

"Is there someone who got burned worse than the others?" I asked.

Maude thought for a few seconds. "I suppose it would be Elmore Grant. I heard that he lost his house when Axel bought the contract for deed from an estate. Elmore had missed a couple of payments, so Axel went to the heirs and offered them a couple thousand dollars for the contract. They jumped at the chance for quick cash and the next day Axel was in court having Elmore's family evicted. Elmore committed suicide the next week and left his widow, Dotty, with four kids, who had no option other than moving in with her brother and sister-in-law."

"So, where is Elmore's widow now?" Wendy asked.

"You know her, Dotty Hathaway in room 316. She remarried a few years after the whole fiasco."

I was at a loss for words. Dotty was a mousy woman who shunned nearly all the others and rarely participated in any activities unless she was virtually dragged along. She was independently mobile, but certainly not someone I could visualize sticking a knife into Axel. Then, a blinding flash of the obvious struck me.

"Maude, are Dotty's children still in the area?" Maude and Wendy both gave me the slow child look, one that I seemed to be getting way too often since Axel's death.

"Peter, can you recall Dotty ever having a visitor?" Wendy asked.

"Well, um. I guess that I haven't seen anyone visiting her."

Maude leaned heavily on the walker with her left hand and started counting off the children on her right fingers. "The oldest boy was killed in a motorcycle accident when he was sixteen. The second boy had some sexual identity problems and moved to San Francisco. The third was a daughter who claimed that her mother had driven her father to drink and that's what led to his eventual suicide. She married the assistant manager at the Hardware Hank and moved to Omaha when he got to manage stores of his own. The youngest was another son, who moved to Minneapolis and hasn't been north of the I-694/494 loop around the Twin Cities since he left."

"I hate to break up this gathering," Kathy, who'd snuck up behind us, said, "but I got an e-mail from the guy who runs our server. Peter, it appears that you've become suddenly popular and your electronic mailbox is overflowing. He said that the synthesized female voice on your computer has gone hoarse from saying, 'You've got mail' so often."

"The Canadian piper probably got you with a spyware program," Wendy offered, looking at the computer. "I hope you didn't have any credit card information or your Social Security number in a file anywhere."

My cell phone buzzed and I looked at the 800 number on the caller ID that meant nothing to me. I could see that had annoyed Kathy, so I dismissed the call. "I'll deal with the e-mails," I said.

The phone buzzed again. Caller ID showed the same number. I pressed "talk."

"This is Chase Bank making a courtesy call on your VISA account. We've picked up an unusual level of activity and wanted to verify that it was indeed you who was initiating all the charges."

My mind was reeling with the possibilities. It could be a scammer trying to get my account information. It could be someone calling as a practical joke. It could be legitimate.

"Could you tell me what the last charges were?" I asked.

"The last charge was for a horse and saddle, in Craig, Colorado, and the charge before that was for an antique silver tea set from somewhere in Ireland," the voice hesitated. "Do you want to know about any more of the charges?"

"No, that's fine. The last legitimate charge should be at Edgar's Gas Station in Two Harbors, Minnesota, about two days ago," I said. I quickly ran through other possible purchases, but most had been paid for in cash or by check. "The charges you mentioned were not any that I made. Can you put a hold on the card, or cancel it?"

"Certainly," the pleasant voice said. "Can you verify your identity by giving me the last four digits of your Social Security number and your mother's maiden name?"

I supplied my mother's maiden name and was assured that I wouldn't be responsible for any of the bogus charges.

Chapter 14

"So, you are an expert in computer hacking?" I asked Wendy, who was sitting at my computer, her fingers flying over the keys.

"Not really," she replied. "I just spend a little time following some of the news and reading online security tips. When was the last time you let the system update your anti-virus software and malware protection?"

"Huh? I thought all that happened automatically."

Wendy continued to type. "It does an automatic update, but you have to accept it."

"Is that the annoying pop-up that asks me if I can shut down and reboot?"

"That would be the one." Her fingers danced over the keys and then came to a sudden stop. "Uh oh. I don't know where you've been on the Internet, but you're getting slammed with spam."

"What?" I asked as I bent down to look at the screen over her shoulder. The e-mail counter said I had 999 waiting messages. The number was pulsating and I had a sick feeling that each pulse represented an attempt to add more charges to my charge card.

The screen changed as Wendy sped between sites and views. "I think you maxed out the available memory on the server when you got to 999 messages. There, I reset the maximum in-box size." She stopped at another screen and I watched as the computer "pinged" as new messages blinked up on the screen faster than a stock exchange ticker.

"Man, look at those subject lines," I said as the string of e-mails scrolled down the screen. Most were offering Viagra, or some kind of male enhancement aids, followed by travel offers, information on cremation services, fake Rolex watches, and re-sale of timeshare condos.

Wendy's fingers spun their magic once again and the list stopped. Suddenly, the number dropped in increments of hundreds. "I started to screen the topics by keywords and the server is blocking some of the most blatant. There, we're down to a mere couple hundred."

She heaved herself out of the chair and pushed it over to me. "However, if you ever want to order Viagra over the Internet, we'll have to change some of the filtering." She gave me a sly smile and added, "You don't need Viagra, do you?"

"Believe me," I said, pointing to the door, "you will not be the first person I come to with that problem."

I looked at the smaller list and still saw dozens with bag-pipes in the subject line. "Wait! How did I get on the list for all these bagpipe e-mails?"

Wendy stepped back into my tiny office and looked at the screen. "Go to your out-box."

When I clicked on the "sent" icon a list of my recent outgoing correspondence popped up. I didn't send many e-mails, so I was surprised to see more than a dozen with today's date.

I quickly scanned the list of subjects and recipients. "I didn't send any of these," I said pointing to the screen.

"Do you have a password on your screen-saver?" Wendy asked.

My blank look answered her question and she quickly took over the keyboard again. Within seconds we were prompted for a password. Wendy looked at me expectantly.

"Um, how about JENNY?" I asked.

I was getting very tired of the "slow child" look. "What?" I asked, defensively.

"Passwords are worthless if any idiot can guess them. You need something that's not obvious and not personal. It's even better if you put some special symbols or numbers into them."

"Special symbols like smiley faces?"

I got the look again as she pointed to the symbols above the numbers at the top of the keyboard.

I contemplated the options for a moment. "Make it s-t-a-r-*-p-o-u-n-d-#" I said.

"Not very creative," she said as she keyed in my new password, "but if you can remember that, it works."

I reclaimed my chair and computer and quickly scanned the outgoing e-mails again, opening two with the subject bagpiper. To my horror, I saw that whoever had been on my computer had offered up my credit card number, with expiration date. I quickly went back through outgoing e-mails and found one that I'd sent with credit card information to secure a reservation for a weekend trip that Jenny and I had made to Grand Marais. The thief had been in my computer's memory, and I'd been too trusting. Leaving the computer without password protection had been like leaving an open checkbook to cyberspace.

Chapter 15

Having lost most of the afternoon on the computer, I went looking for Jenny after shutting down the computer and locking my office. That alone was no easy feat because I had to search for ten minutes to find the key that had never previously been in the lock. Such is the level of trust in Two Harbors, and Whistling Pines. Of course, it was all for strangers and residents, because anyone with a passkey could still enter, and all the staff members had passkeys.

Jenny was charting some patient data, oblivious to the world, when I stuck my head into her office.

"Hey, do you have any supper plans?"

She looked so tired it was concerning. "I guess I hadn't thought that far ahead yet," she said, pushing a stray lock of hair behind her ear. Her desk was piled with patient charts and I could see a stack of pink note slips left by the housekeeping people and the health aides. Behind her was a locked gray cabinet that held the medications for the residents who couldn't manage their own dosing. Open patient charts were strewn on a counter on the opposite wall.

"I thought I'd pick up a couple of Marie Callender turkey potpies and a half-gallon of milk. Care to join me for a gourmet supper?" I asked, trying to put on my best upbeat persona.

Jenny sighed and looked at the chart on her lap. "I don't know, Peter. I just don't think that I can do anything extra tonight. I need to finish up these charts and get home to help Jeremy with his homework."

I walked over and set the chart aside before pulling her into my arms. "It's Axel, isn't it?"

She nodded. "Half the residents are sad, not that they liked Axel, but any death reminds them of their own mortality," Jenny said, her nose buried in my chest. "The other half are excited about the funeral. It seems so morbid, but I guess they don't register the sadness; they're just excited about an outing with a meal."

"Tell you what," I said, holding her by the shoulders. "You finish up here, I'll buy three potpies, and by the time you get to my house, supper will be in the oven and Jeremy and I will be grinding through pre-algebra. Deal?"

All Jenny could muster was a weak smile and a nod.

Jenny and Jeremy live with her parents in a newer house with a brick façade and a cement driveway, which puts them much further up the food chain than most of the people in town. Pulling into their driveway always made me feel like I was going to meet June and Ward Cleaver. No paint was peeling, the lawn was lush and never in need of mowing, and arbor vitae bushes on either side of the front steps were always neatly trimmed and symmetrical.

Barbara, Jenny's mother, met me at the door before I'd climbed the first of the three steps, as she always did. It's surreal, like she has an early warning system, or maybe she sits at the front window all day long watching the wide avenue that goes through their development.

Barbara was trim, with many facial features that had been passed on to Jenny. She was dressed in a pair of khaki slacks that looked like they might be still warm from the iron. Her white blouse was accented with a string of black pearls that I suspected were from Tahiti. As always, her makeup was perfect and her nails manicured.

"Peter, how nice to see you," she said as she stepped back from the door to let me into the house, carefully giving no hints that a hug might be welcome. The tone of her voice didn't match her words.

"Jeremy is gathering his books. I suspect he'll be down in a moment."

I stood on the marble tiles in the entryway, next to the neat row of carefully polished shoes that were always left at the door, never to stray onto the white carpet. The exception to the rule was a pair of stained Nike basketball shoes with flagging laces that had been shed haphazardly on the seam of the carpet and tile. Jeremy obviously ignored the strict order of the household, although he had capitulated to the requirement to remove his shoes.

I was about to comment about the cool weather, that being an always-safe topic, when I heard the rumble of running feet above me. Within seconds, Jeremy was bouncing down the steps two at a time with a backpack slung over one shoulder.

"Jeremy, you'll ruin your back if you don't put both straps on your shoulders," Barbara scolded.

Jeremy jammed his feet into the shoes and pushed past me. "Okay, Gramma," he muttered in passing. I watched him race to my car.

Barbara sighed as she watched him leave. "I'm too young to have a teenaged grandchild, and too old to keep up with him." She turned to me and hesitated. "You know that he thinks the world of you. Please don't disappoint him."

"What do you mean?"

Barbara put her hand on the door in the international symbol for "You are about to leave now," and took a half breath. "I think you know very well what I mean." With the slightest pressure on my elbow I was politely ushered out the door.

As I walked down the steps I reflected on the fact that Barbara didn't have a wrinkle or line anywhere on her face. I'd never seen her frown, scowl, or smile. Apparently that left a person with skin unblemished by the emotions of life. I started to wonder if she was an alien, or if she was just on a good regimen of drugs that subdued all her emotions. On the other hand, she had Scandinavian blood coursing through her veins, and their stoicism was nurtured through many generations. I'd attended a gospel concert at the Swedish Lutheran Church one Friday night and was amazed at the congregational lack of response to the rocking beats. A few people were tapping their toes, but I was the only one who actually stood up and started clapping my hands while swaying to the beat. Some choir members joined me after a few bars, but the majority of the folks stayed politely in the seats, content to let the crazy music people swing to the gospel beat.

Chapter 16

With the fragrance of turkey potpies getting stronger, Jeremy and I sat at the kitchen table and worked our way through his pre-algebra assignment. I'd done well in school, but math wasn't my favorite subject. Having taken algebra a decade before, I found myself searching the recesses of my memory to recall the equations that Jeremy needed to solve the problems.

After solving a number of problems based on simple equations, Jeremy got to the word problem at the end of the assigned questions. Jeremy and I read the inevitable question about two trains traveling toward each other at different speeds.

"Why do they make us do word problems?" Jeremy asked, pushing the book away. "I know how to do all the problems just fine, and then they put this stupid word question in and I'm lost."

"Well, Jeremy," I said, pulling the book back, "in the real world no one will ask you to solve for X and give you the equation. There will be some problem that they throw out, like how long will it take to get a spaceship to Mars, orbit three times, and return to earth. You'll have to put the numbers in to make the equation, and then you'll have to get the answer."

Jeremy squinted at me. "Hello! I don't intend to be a rocket scientist. I just want to pass algebra."

"It doesn't matter what profession you choose, you'll always have word problems that have to be solved."

Our conversation was interrupted by a sound like a firecracker going off just outside my house. There was a second, then a third, immediately followed by the whine of a ricochet. I pulled Jeremy off his chair onto the floor beside me. To the best of my knowledge there had never been a drive-by shooting in Two Harbors, unless you counted poaching deer with a spotlight. I wasn't terribly worried that we were the targets, but ricochets were not particular about who they struck.

"Stay here," I admonished Jeremy, who was shocked at being thrown to the floor. He nodded agreement.

I edged to the window and peeked out just as two more shots rang out. My neighbor, Dolores Karvonen, was standing on her back porch, pointing a rifle into her backyard. After ordering Jeremy again to stay on the floor until I returned, I slipped out the front door and ran to Dolores's house. I slid along the side until I reached the corner where I could see her. Following the angle of the quivering gun barrel, I could see a cottontail rabbit munching on the swelling dogwood buds. Two more shots rang out, hitting landscape rock several feet behind the rabbit, not disturbing him a bit.

"Dolores," I called out. "Hold your fire!"

She turned to look at me, and luckily kept the gun pointed toward the garden. "Peter, come here and shoot that pesky rodent. He's going to kill the dogwoods before they even bud out."

"Point the gun toward the sky and take your finger off the trigger." Once she complied, I climbed over the railing and walked to her side, taking the gun from her hand. In the distance I could hear the wail of a siren.

"You can't shoot rabbits in town," I explained as I removed the shells from the old Remington .22 rifle. "There are houses behind your bushes."

"I know that," she snapped. "I wasn't shooting at the houses. I was shooting at that darned rabbit." The rabbit had moved to a second bush and was nibbling off all the buds within his reach. "If my knees were better I'd be out there chasing him off. But I can't get around anymore, so I found Joe's old varmint gun and decided to deal with it."

The siren stopped a couple blocks away. Within a few seconds I could hear a car door slam in front of the house.

"I think the police are here to talk to you," I said, carefully setting the rifle aside so I didn't appear threatening to the officer. The sound of jingling keys preceded the arrival of Curt Olson, who stopped at the same corner I'd used for cover. His chubby face came into view one eye at a time.

"It's OK, Curt. I've secured the gun."

Dolores strained to see Curt in the fading sunlight. "Is that a cop?" she asked as Curt pulled his sizeable girth over the railing, falling after catching a toe on the way.

"I called you an hour ago about that rabbit, and it's taken you this long to get here," Dolores said sternly. She pointed to the offending rabbit and said, "There he is. Just shoot him and you can leave."

Curt looked at the rabbit, looked at me, and then looked at Dolores. "I'm here because of the gunshots, not the rabbit," Curt explained.

"Well, as long as you're here, you might as well shoot the rabbit," Dolores said, with her hands on her hips.

Curt dusted himself off and said, "Mrs. Karvonen, we had a call that someone was shooting over here. One of the shots nicked the Postens' cat on the ear. I guess that cat was spinning like a whirling dervish, and then dove under their porch. Now he won't come out and I'm here to make sure there isn't any more shooting."

I nodded toward the rusty old gun. "It's no longer loaded."

"Well, someone else must've shot that worthless cat," Dolores said in a huff. "I was only shooting at the rabbit. The cat probably deserved it. They're always into something. If the cat had been worth anything at all, it would've chased that rabbit out of here long ago." Dolores glared at Curt for a second, then asked, "Are you going to shoot the rabbit now?"

"I can't discharge my firearm inside the city limits unless someone's life is in danger," Curt said, picking up the rifle to make sure it wasn't loaded.

"He's killing my dogwoods!" Dolores yelled. "Are you blind?"

Curt's eyes were almost pleading when he looked to me for support. I walked down the steps and across the yard, noting all the little tufts of grass that had been turned up by the errant bullets. When I was about ten feet away, the rabbit bolted.

"There! See how Peter did that? At least someone is willing to take decisive action." Dolores reached for her rifle but Curt pulled it away.

"I'm sorry, ma'am, but I have to confiscate your gun. You can't shoot inside the city limits and the county attorney will probably ask us to give you a ticket for reckless discharge of a firearm."

I shook my head. "There weren't any witnesses, Curt. There wasn't any shooting going on when you got here, and I'm sure I didn't see anything in this fading light, either."

"Do you have any children who might be willing to take care of your rifle, Mrs. Karvonen?" Curt asked.

"Joe and I were never blessed with children. I'll take the gun back."

"You know," I said to Dolores, "if you let me keep the gun for you, I could try to keep the rabbits out of your dogwoods."

"It seems that the sights weren't working too well because I kept missing the stupid rabbit. Maybe you can get them fixed and then we can shoot that rabbit." With that, she turned and went into the house.

"Man," Curt said. "that was scary. Did you see how thick her glasses are? I'm amazed that she could see that there were sights on the gun."

"I don't think she can," I responded. "I'm surprised she could see the rabbit. How's your investigation of Axel Olson's death going?" I asked Curt.

"I don't get into it much. Len seems to be frustrated at the lack of leads. But I think he's kinda hoping that you come up with something from the residents and staff."

"There are a lot of people at the residence who didn't have much time for Axel, and not many who are going to shed a tear at the funeral, but I don't think that I've found anyone who hated him enough to kill him."

"I think the Axel Olson fan club was pretty small," Curt agreed as we stopped on the cracked sidewalk in front of my house. "I remember him sitting in the café with a cribbage board and a deck of cards. He'd play for quarters and I don't think I ever saw him leave with fewer quarters than he started with. I saw a trucker throw the whole deck of cards at Axel after getting double-skunked. Axel just smiled and asked for his winnings. Everyone was pretty sure he was cheating, but no one could ever figure out how."

Chapter 17

I found Jeremy sitting in front of the television with the oven timer buzzing in the kitchen. "How long ago did the buzzer go off?" I called to Jeremy as I searched drawers trying to find a hot pad.

"What buzzer?" He yelled back from the living room.

I shut the buzzer off and pulled the oven door open. "That buzzing sound coming out of my timer saying that the potpies are done."

"I didn't hear it until you turned it off," he replied.

The potpies were a little over-browned, but not burned. That was a major accomplishment in my culinary attempts. I heard Jenny open the front door as I pulled the last potpie from the oven.

"Peter, why is there a gun leaning against the coat rack and can you make it go away?"

"Don't worry, it's not loaded," I replied. "I'll take it to the basement as soon as I turn off the oven."

"Cool. What kind of gun is it?" Jeremy asked as I whisked it away a second before he tried to pick it up. "Is that the one from the drive-by shooting?"

"What drive-by shooting?" Jenny asked. The concern in her voice stopped me in my tracks.

"There was no drive-by shooting," I said calmly.

"Then why did we have to duck and cover?" Jeremy asked, being a typical, non-helpful tween.

"Dolores, my next door neighbor, was shooting at a rabbit in her backyard. That's all it was," I said as I started down the basement stairs. "And I thought I told you to stay on the floor until I got back," I said to Jeremy.

"You were gone a long time," Jeremy replied, "and there wasn't any more shooting."

"She shot a rabbit in her backyard, right next to your house?" Jenny yelled down the basement stairwell.

I slid the gun into the rafters and started back up the stairs. "No. She shot at a rabbit. She didn't hit it."

"Why is she shooting at rabbits in town?" Jenny's patience was wearing thin, and my efforts to minimize the situation weren't effective.

"She shot at him because he was eating her dogwood bushes," I replied as I pulled plates from the cupboard and set three places at the table. "It really wasn't a big deal. She was shooting into the ground."

"Yeah," Jeremy jumped in. "Except for the cool ricochet. Ziiingggg! It sounded just like they do on the cop shows."

I tried to give Jeremy a "Shut up!" look, but I just didn't have the power in my glare. Or maybe my look was being cancelled out by the look I was getting from Jenny.

"So, is that the only gun Dolores has?" Jenny asked as she set out silverware.

"I'm sure it is," I replied, realizing too late that there was no conviction in my voice.

Jenny was on the way to the door before I could pour glasses of milk. "C'mon, Peter, we're going to see if she has any other guns."

"But, supper," I said to her back as she stepped out the door.

For a small person with short legs, Jenny moved fast when her adrenaline was flowing. Maybe it was the adrenaline, or maybe it was the lioness instinct to protect her cub. Either way, she was knocking on Dolores's door before I hit the bottom step. When the door opened, we were side-by-side.

"Peter and Ginny, how nice of you to stop over," Dolores said, beaming at the prospect of company.

"Actually, her name is Jenny," I said to Dolores's back as she took Jenny by the elbow and led her into the sitting room.

Dolores put Jenny in one of two matching upholstered chairs with carved arms and brocade covers. I was left standing at the edge of a beautiful ivory and burgundy wool rug that was probably hand tied when Iran was still called Persia. I wandered over to an old roll-top desk that appeared to be solid teak. The matching chair creaked as I sat down, then nearly flipped me over backwards when I leaned back.

"Oh, Peter, stop being such a clown," Dolores admonished me. "Joe used to do that same trick for laughs when we entertained during the war. Could I offer you a glass of sherry?"

"Oh, thank you so much, but we really can't stay very long," Jenny said, making a complete transition from protective lioness to charming guest. "We came over because we are concerned about your guns."

"My guns?" Dolores said, completely surprised.

"Well, yes. Peter is taking care of the one you used to shoot the rabbit," Jenny cooed, "but it's so rusty. I was wondering if you would like Peter to take care of any others that you have so they don't rust and get ruined?"

To say that I was in awe would be an understatement. Seeing Jenny turning her ire into manipulative compassion and concern was eye opening. I'd seen her use smaller doses of this technique at Whistling Pines, but this performance was something to behold.

"Why yes," Dolores responded. She turned her head, as if in thought, then said, "Let's see what shape the others are in. I haven't been in that cabinet in years."

She led us up the stairs and into a bedroom with a canopy bed that looked like something out of a museum. The matching furniture was exquisitely carved walnut with a dark varnish finish. The bedspread and canopy appeared to be matching red silk embroidered with gold thread. Near the window was a small cabinet with a marble washbasin, and a ewer that appeared to have been cut from the same marble.

Dolores opened a closet, exposing an armoire that matched the other furniture, with beautiful moose and elk carvings cut into the front panels. She removed a small key from a hook on the side of the cabinet and unlocked the doors. When she opened them, she revealed an amazing collection of pistols hanging from the doors and long guns standing inside the cabinet.

"I don't know a lot about guns," she said, stepping back from the cabinet. She pointed to one. "My father gave Joe this gun for a wedding present. He called it a Purdy, or something like that, and Joe was quite impressed. He always said that he couldn't bear to shoot the thing for fear of ruining it."

I looked into the cabinet and saw the gun she was pointing to. It was an old double-barreled shotgun with external hammers and gold inlays depicting pheasants on the wing. The other long guns appeared to be of the same vintage, and the pistols were nearly all made for black powder and looked very old.

Dolores saw me staring at a pistol and redirected my gaze. "I don't know much about most of these, but I think this one was my grandfather's from the Civil War. He commanded company C of the 3rd Minnesota volunteer regiment who laid siege to Vicksburg. His sword is over here, in the corner."

"Um, Dolores," I said, searching for words. "These belong in a museum." I picked up a badly battered pistol that didn't seem to fit with the rest of the carefully oiled pristine firearms.

"That odd one that you're looking at," she said, pointing to the worn piece with all the bluing worn off, "that was given to my father by General Pershing after World War I. He told daddy that he'd bought it from a Mexican bartender who claimed that it had been taken from the dead hand of Jim Bowie after the Mexicans overran the Alamo. I've never put much stock in that, but it was so special to my father that I felt we should keep it."

I gently replaced the scarred pistol, closed and locked the cabinet, and slipped the key on a ring with my house key. "I'll hold this key for safekeeping."

Jenny gently led Dolores from the room, using the same gentle elbow nudge that her mother had used on me earlier in the day. "We should contact your relatives so they're aware of this historical collection," she suggested.

"Oh, that's not necessary," Dolores explained as we went down the stairs. "My mother died in childbirth, and my father could never bear the thought of losing another wife, so he never married again. Joe had two brothers who were killed in the Pacific during the war, and Joe and I were never blessed with children. So, you see, there really is no family to pass this on to."

"Well, we certainly need to contact your insurance agent to make sure you have adequate coverage for all your valuables," Jenny suggested.

Dolores made a frown. "Joe didn't believe in insurance. He said, 'Put the premiums in your pocket and in ten years you'll be money ahead.' We've lived by that credo. All those premiums that we've never paid amount to a tidy sum of money."

"I guess it's a generational thing," I said with a shrug. "Just like Axel Olson. He never put a penny in a bank because he didn't trust them, and didn't want them making money off his money."

Dolores's eyes narrowed. "Axel Olson was a bounder of the highest order."

"A bounder?" I asked.

"He tried long ago to swindle Joe on a land deal. Joe got wise to him and turned the tables on him. It could've been tough for us except that everyone else in the area knew about Axel and his shady business. Axel hired an attorney out of Minneapolis, because no one up here would touch anything that had to do with him. The judge in town almost laughed him out of the courtroom. You should've seen that Minneapolis attorney. His face was the color of a cooked beet after the tongue-lashing he got from the judge."

"Did anyone else ever get the best of Axel?" Jenny asked.

"There was one guy that came to us after we got through with the court case. I don't remember his name, but he was the moneyman in a project where Axel was supplying the brains and taking most of the profit. He came and met with Joe, and I think that he left with some ideas about how to handle Axel. It's a pity that the poor man was killed in a duck hunting accident the next week. His boat tipped over and he drowned or froze to death, as I remember it."

Chapter 18

Wednesday

On Wednesday morning the names on the new, expanded sign-up sheets for transportation to Axel's funeral overran the available space. Little old people with shaking hands, trained in the spiky Palmer method of handwritten script, made for difficult reading at best. Some wrote their names in the margins of the paper and deciphering the names became as difficult as solving the Cryptoquip in the *Duluth News Tribune.* After fifteen minutes I gave up and assumed that every resident who didn't own a car was going to need a ride.

Carolyn Young, the transportation coordinator for the Two Harbors Unified School District, said she needed the school buses on school-day afternoons. They could not let me rent even one bus for the funeral. She was very cordial, but I could tell that I was getting the "Are you stupid?" treatment by the tone of her voice.

I tried calling a tour bus service in Duluth, but both of their buses were already booked with tours to Branson,

Missouri. I was Googling "bus" and "Duluth" when I heard the whisper of cloth rubbing against cloth a moment before a shadow blocked the light coming through my office door.

"Are you still searching for bagpipes?" Wendy asked, trying to peek over my shoulder at the computer screen.

I clicked off the monitor and turned to face her. There really wasn't anything to hide, but I knew that a hidden screen would drive her crazy with curiosity. "Do you have someone?"

"No, but we're only days away from the funeral and the person responsible for the music," she said, pointing at me, "has a big hole in the program where there's supposed to be music. All the little old ladies believe that there will be bagpipes playing, and right now, it looks like it will be filled with you singing a cappella."

"First of all, we are jointly responsible for the music and you will be either performing or accompanying the performer of our choice. I am trying to find bagpipes." I turned the screen on, illuminating the bus search screen. "Secondly, if I don't find a bus to haul our residents it looks like I'll be making laps with the van for a couple hours."

"My cousin has a bus," Wendy said, looking at the screen. "It looks a lot like that, only without windows." She pointed at a large tour bus that said it seated 58 people.

"Why does your cousin have a tour bus?"

"Because he tours," she replied sarcastically, adding, "Duh," to the implied insult.

"What kind of tours?" I asked, trying to remain polite.

"He's the driver for The Seasick Sailors." I must've given her my best look of confusion because she added, "They're a polka band. They tour around the Midwest about four months a year."

"So, The Seasick Sailors are not on tour right now and your cousin might be able to drive a couple loads of senior citizens to a funeral?"

"I can ask. The worst that'll happen is that he'll say they're on tour, or that he doesn't want to."

I pushed the phone across the desk to her. "I'm kinda running out of time. Can you call him now?"

Wendy glanced at her watch. "He's not a morning person, and I really don't like to interrupt him when he's, um, entertaining an overnight guest." She looked at the phone nervously.

"Please."

She picked up the phone and dialed the number from memory while I turned to the computer and Googled The Seasick Sailors. Within seconds I had a picture of seven guys, all wearing blue blazers and captain's caps, standing around their instruments. The youngest appeared to be 60. The accordion player looked like he was past 80.

"Enos, this is Wendy. How are you?" Wendy asked as she put the conversation on speakerphone.

"Wendy," the voice sounded very tentative. "I'm doing well. Sorry I didn't call, but you know how things get busy with the band and all."

"This is your cousin Wendy."

"Ohhh, that Wendy," Enos' voice, which sounded a little raspy, like a long-time smoker, almost dripped with relief. "Long time, no see. What can I do for you?"

"I'm guessing that you're still the front man for the band and spending a little time with some of the polka groupies."

"Now, Wendy, groupie is a rather derogatory term. I like to think of them as grateful fans. So, you're calling to check on my love life?"

"I'm working at the Whistling Pines, in Two Harbors, and we've got a problem. We need to drive a bunch of senior citizens from Whistling Pines to a church funeral and I can't find anyone who has a bus available for the funeral.

I was wondering if you could drive the band bus over and ferry a couple loads of senior citizens for us?"

When Enos' answer didn't jump from the phone I whispered, "Tell him we could pay a hundred dollars."

"Do I need to drive to the cemetery?"

"No, we just need to get two busloads from Whistling Pines to the Lutheran Church."

"Lutherans. Hmm. Are they catering lunch?"

Wendy put up a finger and leaned close to the speakerphone. "The Lutheran ladies are catering lunch themselves. I heard that they're doing ham sandwiches, salads, and cakes. I'm sure they'll have a couple Jell-O salads, too."

"You know, Jell-O salads aren't a big draw for me anymore. The last Baptist funeral I went to had a lime Jell-O salad with canned peas floating in it. Can't say that's a recipe that I'd save. Now, if you tell me that there's going to be a tangerine Jell-O salad with Mandarin oranges, well I might be interested in that. Even better would be rice pudding or tapioca pudding, as long as they don't dump a bunch of raisins into it."

"Enos, I'll make a raisin-less rice pudding myself if you'll drive the bus."

"You know, the band isn't booked. I could call the guys and we could play for the dance," Enos offered.

"Uh, Enos, this is a funeral, not a wedding," Wendy said.

"There are bands at funerals. Haven't you ever seen an Irish wake?" Enos asked.

"Enos, these are Swedish Lutherans. We can barely get them to sway with the funeral music, much less dance. Besides, they don't play polkas at Irish wakes."

"Say, is this the Friday funeral with the bagpipes?" he asked. "I've never seen a bagpiper. I'd be willing to drive for nothing if you've got live bagpipes."

"It's a deal!" Wendy said as I flapped my arms, trying to stop her from making the promise. "I'll see you at eleven Friday."

"How can you promise him bagpipes?" I squawked as she punched off the speakerphone. "I don't have bagpipes coming. I don't even have the prospect of bagpipes."

"Peter, don't have a heart attack. By the time Enos gets everyone to the church it'll be too late for him to turn back." Wendy spun and walked out the door.

"I need him to drive them back here after the funeral, too!" I yelled at her back.

I almost bowled over Len Rentz as I rushed through the door. "Who's driving back from the funeral?" he asked.

"Wendy's cousin, Enos, is driving The Seasick Sailors' band bus to the funeral. He's going to bring a couple loads of residents to the Lutheran Church."

"They own that big red bus that has 'Oom-Pah-Pah' written across the sides. I've seen them play a couple times and they put on quite a show. You could do worse than having them play at the funeral." Len paused a beat and then asked, "Are you getting them instead of the bagpiper?"

"No, there is no bagpiper and The Seasick Sailors won't be playing, either."

"It's probably just as well that you're not having the band. They really were Great Lakes sailors, and they tend to be a little randy at times. From what I hear, they could've given Axel philandering lessons. You know that old saying about musicians?"

I suddenly had a very disturbing picture of the seven Seasick Sailors chasing my little old ladies around with carnal intentions. The scariest part was that most of my residents would be flattered.

"No, I don't know the saying about musicians, and I don't care to," I replied, letting my overall irritation spill onto Len. "Did you have something special, Len? I'm way behind with the funeral plans and I don't have time for idle chatter right now."

"How are you doing with the inside snooping job?" Len asked. He pulled a pipe and tobacco pouch from his pocket.

"You can't smoke in here. It's a state law."

Len clamped the unlit pipe in his teeth and inhaled deeply with his eyes closed. "I know, but sometimes I just need to get a whiff of tobacco to get the rush."

I shook my head. "I think that means that you're not physically addicted."

"It makes no difference whether it's psychological or physical, I still want it." Len folded the tobacco pouch and put it back into his pocket. "Back to my original question. What have you heard?" he asked, the pipe still clenched between his teeth.

"I had an interesting talk with my neighbor, Dolores," I said, leading Len into my office and closing the door behind us. "It seems that she and her late husband got the best of Axel in court after a land deal went south on them. She said that someone came to them after that to get some direction on dealing with Axel. I guess the guy had some plans but he mysteriously died in a duck hunting accident."

"Yeah," Len said, "I know about Hank Cook. The coroner ruled his death an accidental drowning, although I think he didn't look much further once he found water in the victim's lungs."

"Was there more to investigate?"

"I thought it odd that Axel Olson was in the boat with Hank but didn't even get damp during his attempted rescue efforts, especially considering that Axel and Hank were in the middle of a contentious court fight."

"Hank went duck hunting with Axel when they were fighting in court?" I asked. "That does seem odd."

"Yup, even Hank's wife was surprised. She thought he was going hunting alone, and was more than surprised that he was with Axel. She said they didn't even like to eat ducks."

"Has anyone else given you any other insights?" Len asked, once more fidgeting with the pipe, moving it from one side of his mouth to the other.

"I've been a little busy with my job. The funeral planning is really chewing me up. Everybody seems to want something and they think that tomorrow will be too late."

"Hmm," Len said, looking at my screensaver flashing irregular patterns that reminded me of the northern lights. "I got a call back from one of Stella's Finnish visitors this morning. He was the guy who made all the arrangements for the Great Lakes tour and made sure that everyone made it to the buses and the boat on time. The actual date of Stella's birthday party was dictated by when their boat docked in Duluth. He'd arranged for a van to drive them to Two Harbors. Most of the Finns were Stella's octogenarian cousins with a couple younger people to assist with the canes, walkers, oxygen bottles, and wheelchairs."

"They don't sound like the kind of people who'd be murderers."

Len smiled. "I learned a long time ago that appearances deceive."

"I don't suppose he told you that one of his people killed Axel?"

"Actually, his response was, 'Who is this Axel person?' I explained Axel's Finnish link and he said that he'd never heard of Axel. They had quite an experience after they left

Duluth. The ship was struck with some stomach virus and nearly half the passengers and crew were down with miserable intestinal distress that held them up in Thunder Bay for two days while they washed the whole ship with disinfectant."

"I read that in the newspaper. I hope they didn't spread any of the virus around here or the state Health Department will have this place quarantined so fast it'll make your head spin."

There was a quiet knock on the door and Len had to sit down in my lone visitor chair so I could squeeze past him. I was surprised to see Howard Johnson standing there with a look of concern.

"Peter, I know that you're busy with the funeral plans, but something has come up that needs your attention." Dozens of terrible situations passed through my mind during Howard's short pause. "A number of the ladies are concerned that they don't have appropriate clothing for a spring funeral and they need you to take them in the van to Duluth so they can shop at the mall."

Len chuckled as he stuck his face around the door. "In the greater scheme of things, a trip to the mall isn't much of an emergency."

"You go down and explain that to a dozen angry hens," Howard replied tersely.

I patted Howard on the arm and said, "Tell them that I'm busy, but I promise that I will find someone to drive them to Duluth tomorrow afternoon."

"Thank you, Peter. I'm not entirely sure how I was elected to deliver this message, but I'm certain that my afternoon would've been miserable if you hadn't given the OK."

"Howard, would the ladies have put Axel up to a chore like this?" Len asked.

Howard snorted. "They wouldn't ask Axel for the time of day. He had a tendency to give ungentlemanly responses to anything that might inconvenience him."

"So, Axel wasn't just tight with his money?" Len asked.

"Oh, no, Axel didn't want to be involved in anything that didn't benefit Axel. In his mind, minor inconveniences were major annoyances, and he tended to suffer with profane tirades to spread his pain to as many innocent bystanders as possible."

"I'm surprised he ever left his room," Len observed.

"You don't understand Axel," Howard explained. "He had to be around people, making himself appear superior, always more important. If we sang in the community room, we sang his choice of songs. When we watched television, we watched what Axel wanted to see at the volume Axel wanted to hear it. If someone was talking nearby while Axel was watching television, he turned the volume up until he couldn't hear them, or until they left."

"Axel wouldn't play bingo," I added, "because he didn't win all the time. When he lost, he tended to throw the cards and storm out."

"I'm surprised that someone didn't throw him out," Len said.

"I'm surprised that someone didn't kill him long ago," Howard replied as he turned and walked away.

"Howard!" Len called after the departing senior. "Is there anyone who didn't play along with Axel's drama?"

"Didn't play along? I don't understand your question."

"It sounds like most of you were too polite to call Axel on his behavior. Is there someone who wouldn't play along with his dramatics?" Len said. "You know, someone who just walked away when Axel showed up, or showed particular animosity toward him?"

Howard seemed to be dumbstruck by the question. Slowly, a smile crossed his face. "I see. You want to know if there is someone who is the strong silent type. You're not worried about the baying Bassets among us, you want to find the silent killer who doesn't act out, kind of like a guard dog who doesn't bark, just bites."

"The canine metaphor aside, is there someone who didn't put up with Axel's antics?" Len asked. "Is there someone who quietly slipped away when Axel became profane?"

"There are a number of women who don't socialize much in the common areas, but I doubt that they stay in their rooms to avoid Axel. A couple of the men tend to stay in their rooms to watch television without the background noise downstairs. A few people are just introverted and don't feel comfortable in the groups downstairs and aren't seen except at mealtime."

"Most of the women who work in the dining room wouldn't turn their backs on him," I offered. "He pinched or groped most of them, so they tended to back away from him when they served his table. Angie growled at him when she got near him and she made it pretty clear that she wouldn't put up with his nonsense, and Miriam almost broke his wrist when he put his hand on her thigh."

"Is Angie the cook with the tattoos?" Len asked.

"Yup," I replied.

"I've met her, and I think she'd slap him silly or give him a piece of her mind rather than waiting until he was alone and then killing him. We're looking for someone who's more like a pressure cooker, someone who keeps it all pent up inside until one day he just blew and killed Axel."

"I don't know who that would be," Howard replied.

Chapter 19

I looked for Wendy, hoping to coerce her into driving the van to Duluth for the shopping outing. As usual, Wendy was never to be found when I needed her. I found her in the hair salon chatting with the stylist and Edith McIlroy, who was getting a lavender tint.

"Wendy, could you do me a favor?" Since Wendy was the assistant director, I had to couch my request as a favor.

"Peter, the last time I did you a favor, I ended up fishing Edna's dentures out of the toilet. Not that it did any good. She never put them back in her mouth again anyway."

"I'm up to my eyeballs in the funeral plans and I need you to drive the van to Duluth tomorrow. A few of the women want to buy new funeral clothes."

"Will I have to babysit them, or can I just turn them loose and do some shopping of my own?" Wendy asked.

"I usually drop the people off at the Herbergers' entrance and tell everyone to synchronize watches. We meet at the same entrance in two hours and I spend the time in the music shop looking for new songbooks and guitars. Fifteen minutes before the departure time I retrieve the van and park at the same drop point. The people straggle out with their bags and I help them get loaded back on the van. Some return exhausted and a little early, and some others show up a couple minutes late."

"They are independent and unsupervised?" Wendy asked. "I don't want to spend my afternoon babysitting. Most of all, I don't want surprises."

"Hey, what can go wrong with a van full of senior citizens?" I joked. "Take your book of *New York Times* crossword puzzles and relax at the coffee kiosk. I'll leave the van keys on my desk."

"I hear my name came up in the murder investigation."

I recognized Angie's raspy voice at my office door. "You came up only in the context that you were one of the people who actually stood up to Axel, not as a suspect," I replied, pushing away from the computer.

"Well, that's good, because I wouldn't kill anyone." She stood leaning against the doorframe with her arms crossed. She wore a stained white apron, a short-sleeved white blouse and white jeans. Her rose tattoo showed on her right wrist. The butterfly on her other wrist was hidden under her folded arms. The stud in her nose and the safety pin through her eyebrow were distracting. I had to try hard not to stare at them when we spoke.

"I think we know that."

Angie gave an emphatic nod. "Good. I'm glad we're clear on that." She continued to stand in the doorway with her arms crossed.

"Is there something else?" I asked, glancing back at my computer, thinking about all the work I had left to do.

"Axel had something else going on." I waited for her to go on. "He was rich, you know, so a lot of the residents were asking him about ways to make money. I think that he may've been investing money for them."

Most of the residents were retired railroad workers, farmers, and their wives who were living off Social Security and meager savings. "Oh, man. I thought we had enough suspects with the folks around town that Axel had crossed," I moaned.

"Don't forget whoever he's been screwing."

"You've heard the rumors? Do you think they're true?"

"I know that the kitchen staff have seen women sneaking in and out of his room when they delivered meals to sick residents or when they picked up the dishes."

"Do you have any names?"

"I'm not a tattletale," she replied over her shoulder as she left.

I turned to the computer and polished off the activity schedule for the following week and printed it. After posting the schedule in the lobby, I realized that a headache was starting to creep into my forehead. I tried to remember if I'd had any caffeine, and decided that I was probably two cups behind on my daily ration of coffee. Wendy looked up from her crossword puzzle as I drew a cup of coffee from the urn near the kitchen.

"I need a nine-letter word for beggar," she said, tapping her pencil on the tabletop. "I tried panhandler, but that's ten letters."

"Mendicant," I replied, as I poured a dollop of cream into the coffee. I knew the coffee wouldn't help much because it looked and smelled like coal tar. I suspected that all the caffeine had been burned out.

Wendy looked at me skeptically. "How do you spell it?"

"M-e-n-d-i-c-a-n-t," I replied

She wrote the letters down as I spoke them and then stared at the puzzle. "Peter, why do you know that word?"

"I missed it in the sixth-grade spelling bee," I replied. "It's etched indelibly in my memory like a childhood scar."

"Hmmph," If that's your worst scar your childhood was pretty mild. Pre-teen girls are vicious. They're all terribly insecure and they try to feel better by making someone else's life miserable."

"It doesn't stop at teens," Jenny added, having swept into the room behind my back. "Adult women can be catty, too."

"Isn't it nice that the high-paid staff gets to sit around drinking coffee and talking about teen insecurities when there are a hundred people, who rely on you, roaming the hallways unsupervised?"

I didn't recognize the middle-aged man who had walked into the dining room. He was around 60 years old, with a halo of frizzy white hair ringing his bald pate. He wore a white shirt that strained to hold his ample stomach, and a pair of khaki pants. The only discordant portion of his attire was a pair of reddish-brown stained work boots, which hinted that he had something to do with the iron mining industry.

"Can I help you, sir?" Jenny asked.

"I think it's a little late for that," he replied. "If you'd been more watchful, my father might still be alive." He limped into the room, favoring his left leg and grimacing with each step. He pulled a chair from the table nearest us and sat down.

"Can I get you a cup of coffee, Mr. Olson?" Wendy asked as she slipped the crossword puzzle under the table-cloth.

"That would be the least you could do at this point," the man replied.

This must be Axel Olson's middle child, I thought. I'd never seen him in person. None of Axel's children had ever previously darkened the halls of Whistling Pines.

"Are you Daryl Olson?" I asked. "I recall your father speaking about you."

"My name is Darren," the man replied with disdain, "and I doubt that my father ever mentioned me." He paused for a second, then added, "Unless my name was preceded by a string of expletives."

Wendy handed Darren Olson a cup of coffee and he took it from her hand with a look that he might've given a leper. He didn't bother to thank her.

"I suppose you must be Peter, the incompetent idiot who's trying to find someone to play bagpipes at Axel's funeral. Len Rentz suggested that I stop here to talk to you."

If anyone else had addressed me like that, I would've been insulted, but in the case of Darren Olson, it was easy to consider the source and dismiss the insult.

"Mr. Olson, are you here to provide some input on the funeral arrangements?" Jenny asked, trying to redirect the conversation.

"If it was up to me, he'd be cremated and his ashes scattered at the landfill. No, I wouldn't make the trip to the landfill: it'd be easier just to put the ashes into the garbage and let the truck take them there."

Even I was struck dumb and I looked to Jenny, whose mouth was gaping. Wendy was the only one who had a response.

"We've reserved the Lutheran church for the funeral," she said.

Darren made a face like he'd sucked a lemon. "If you can find a church that'll take him, either alive or dead, go for it." He paused as he was obviously framing his thoughts, and then added, "It seems like whatever building a coven uses for meetings would be more fitting. I don't know what you'd call that, maybe a witch's cave?"

"Lutherans are pretty tolerant," Wendy said.

"I don't need your flippant sarcasm," Darren said, rising from the chair with great effort. "I'll be at the church, but don't expect me, or any of my siblings, to shed any tears."

As Darren Olson walked out the door, Wendy turned to Jenny and me. "I think that went pretty well, don't you?" She sat down, picked up her pencil, and started looking at the crossword puzzle as if the issue was decided.

I looked at Jenny, who was actually looking a little sad. "I don't appreciate people who air their family's dirty laundry."

"You missed the conversation I had with Axel's daughter," I said. "It went much the same way."

Jenny closed her eyes. "I don't think I can deal with this stress over the funeral. My stomach is in knots; I'm getting by on three or four hours of sleep worrying about a murderer roaming the halls."

Wendy, apparently oblivious to our conversation, was tapping her pencil, in deep thought over something in the crossword. "Blackberry brandy," she suddenly blurted.

"What?" I asked.

"Jenny needs blackberry brandy. It settles your stomach and helps you sleep," Wendy said, and then added, "It also helps with irregularity."

Jenny leaned close and whispered, "That man seemed angry enough to be a murderer."

I nodded and thought Darren would be near the top of the suspect list.

Chapter 20

The smell of pipe tobacco wafted through my office, preceding Len's arrival. "Anything new?"

"Axel's son, Darren, was here today. He's quite a piece of work. He suggested that we have Axel cremated and the ashes hauled away with the garbage."

"The whole family is cracked," Len said. "It's like that Johnny Cash song about a guy who named his son Sue, to harden him in preparation for dealing with the world. From all appearances, that's pretty much what Axel did to all three of his children. He set them all up in businesses, but seemed to wring or extort repayment with usurious interest from them and did all he could to make sure they came close to failing."

"Axel was quite a guy," was all I could add.

"That's not all. He may not have been able to take it with him, but somehow he seems to have tied up or hidden all his money so no one else can get it," Len added.

"I don't understand what you're saying."

"Axel set up some sort of blind trust that ties up all his property and money. No one has the authority to liquidate any of his real estate, nor can they sell any of the securities. If they try to contest the will they are cut out of any inheritance."

"So who wins?"

"I can't figure it out," Len replied. "I've been trying to follow the money, because that is certainly where the biggest motive lies, but it doesn't look like anyone wins right now. There is an interesting clause in Axel's will that directs the trustee to give a million dollar payment to the first of his children who makes a million dollars. Right now, it doesn't appear that any of the children are in a business that will ever make that milestone."

"Who is the trustee?" I asked.

"The lawyer didn't recognize the name. It's a woman from the Twin Cities. He's trying to contact her."

"Money or not," I said, "Darren Olson seemed angry enough to kill someone. Axel's daughter was here earlier, and she was as bitter as Darren, although a lot of her rant had less vitriol than the son's bitterness."

My head was still buzzing from the conversation with Darren Olson and Len's news about Axel's will when I walked to my car after work. The wind had died and the dampness that had chilled me to the bone most of the week had given way to a drier coolness. I thought about all the things that needed to be accomplished before the funeral and felt overwhelmed.

"Snuffy" Saari was polishing his yellow and black '57 Chevy in the residents' parking lot. The ever-present bulging wad of Copenhagen snuff was tucked under his lower lip. He had little color in his life except his Chevy, which he cleaned endlessly. Unlike most of the cars in the lot,

Snuffy's Chevy was free of rust and fender dents except for a severely rumpled rear bumper.

"The car is looking good," I said as I passed.

Snuffy nodded without changing expression. "I'm just glad that we're past the salt season on the roads. That salt is sure hard on the fenders," he replied with his thick Finnish accent as he rubbed a stained towel on a non-existent blemish on the trunk.

"Yeah, but if they don't put salt on the streets, we'd all be playing bumper cars on the ice for six months of the year," I replied, pointing to the twist in his bumper, "kind of like you did there."

Snuffy's expression darkened. "That wasn't no accident," he said, spitting Copenhagen juice for emphasis. He turned away and went back to polishing.

I heard Jenny calling my name. She was hustling across the driveway, her briefcase flopping against her hip. Snuffy was immediately forgotten.

"I think we should go out to the American Legion Hall for dinner tonight. It's pasty night," Jenny said, taking my hand in hers. "And then we can go out to Hugo's to hear Wendy's band."

"I guess that's okay." I tried to remember the last time I'd eaten a pasty, the hearty meat and potato mixture folded in a pie crust. Pasties had been a lunch-bucket staple for the iron range miners and they remained a favorite regional comfort food. "Will they have gravy?"

"Peter, everyone eats ketchup on pasties."

"I like gravy better."

"Get over it. They'll have ketchup."

"What time do we pick up Jeremy?"

"I talked to my mother. She picked him up from school and they're eating fish sticks and green beans, his favorites."

She mistook my lost look for disinterest, and added, "But if you've got other plans…"

"No," I said, a little too sharply. I softened my face and took her other hand in mine. "I was just lost in other thoughts. The funeral planning is eating me up."

Jenny leaned close and brushed her lips against mine. "Let it go for tonight and have dinner with me, then we can drive out to hear Wendy's band."

"Get a room!" Wendy yelled across the parking lot. She was grinning broadly as she climbed into her vintage bright yellow VW beetle.

I traced Jenny's jaw line with the tip of my finger, eliciting a shiver. I kissed the tip of her nose and pulled her close. "We could skip supper and just go back to my place for dessert."

"Nice try, big spender," Jenny said, pushing me toward my car. "I haven't had anything to eat since noon. Feed me or I walk."

"Are we leaving your car here?" I asked.

She turned and smiled at me. "I dropped it off at your house when Wendy and I went out for lunch. That way we can leave some mystery about our relationship among the rumormongers when we drive to work separately in the morning."

"Well, except for Wendy, the head rumormonger."

"Peter, did you ever find a piper?" she asked.

"I didn't find a piper," I said, sighing as I unlocked the door, then cleared the candy wrappers and a Beatle's songbook from the passenger seat of my car.

"There are going to be a lot of disappointed old ladies," Jenny said as she settled into the car and buckled her seatbelt. "What are you going to do for music?"

I started the car and shrugged as I backed out of my parking spot. "I suppose that Wendy and I will do our usual tag team effort. She's got a couple songs she's been practicing and she's going to do a solo after the sermon."

"About that. Wendy told me that she was thinking about doing "Penny Lane" for the solo."

I glanced at Jenny to see if she was smiling. "'Penny Lane'?" I asked. "Do you mean the Beatles song?"

"I'm pretty sure she was talking about the Beatles. She said that it had deep meaning, and she started to talk about the symbolism of the barbershop and the pictures of all the heads that had been shorn."

I suddenly realized why Wendy had borrowed my Beatles song book. I had a terrible vision of two hundred old people looking around at each other, asking what idiot had picked some song about a barbershop for a funeral.

"Do you think she was kidding?" I asked.

"I don't think so. She seemed quite serious about it."

I groaned. "I'd better update my resume."

"It's not that bad," Jenny said, patting my arm. "She was looking for Loch Lomond, and thought that she'd play that on the organ as the recessional, so it sounds like bagpipes."

"I suppose that's better than the 'Tennessee Waltz'."

"Oh, that would be stupid. Who'd use a waltz as a recessional?"

"Can we change the topic?" I asked as I drove toward downtown. "I'd like to relax a little and if we pursue this any further I won't get any sleep tonight."

Jenny leaned her head against my shoulder and put her hand on the inside of my thigh. "I wasn't planning on getting a lot of sleep tonight."

"I kinda liked the idea of skipping right to dessert," I said, feeling a primal response to the location of Jenny's hand.

"I promised Wendy that we'd watch her band tonight. Dessert can wait."

I took Jenny's hand from my thigh and put it on the console. "In that case, it's best if we don't give rise to anything else at the moment."

I drove down First Street and found an empty parking spot around the corner from the American Legion hall. "The Legion" caters to a local crowd of veterans and their guests who come in for inexpensive drinks, comfort food, and local color. As the World War II vets died off, the club opened its doors to "unescorted guests," which meant anyone was welcome, although they retained their official standing as a private club. On Friday and Saturday nights the Legion Auxiliary serves inexpensive evening dinners that vary according to the season. Smelt fries are popular when the smelt swim upriver to spawn in the spring, and all-you-can-eat fish and chips are served every Friday during Lent. My personal favorites are the nights they serve fried chicken or pot roast, although all of it's better than cooking for myself.

At the front door I pushed a doorbell button and nodded to the two Viet Nam-era vets who were smoking next to a "butt disposal station." Minnesota passed an indoor smoking ban and the many vets who smoke are relegated to standing outside the door when they need a nicotine fix. A buzz indicated that the bartender had released the door for us. We walked past the old mailbox, painted red, white, and blue, which is there to collect worn-out American flags the Legion members burn at solemn Flag Day ceremonies. A bar ran the full length of the room and tables, set for foursomes, were spread around the rest of the room. The hard-wood floors are scarred with scrapes and cigarette burns, and the ceiling, which had probably once been white, is now ivory colored from the years of cigarette smoke dating back to WWI.

I chose a table near the kitchen and pulled the chair out for Jenny. A few other Iraq vets were sitting at the bar and they nodded to me. The rest of the faces were regulars I'd seen during my many dinners there. Several smiled or nodded.

Part of the color that night was Dottie, our waitress, who was close to 70 and a fixture at the Legion in the two years I'd been eating there. She barely fit between the tables and wore a flannel shirt and blue jeans. She announced that pasties were the special of the night, and since the cook hadn't made anything else, they were also the only choice. Our options came down to a choice of beverage.

We ordered Leinenkugel's Honeyweiss beer. "Do you have gravy for the pasties?" I asked.

The question garnered a glare from both Dottie and Jenny. Dottie tapped her pen on the order pad a couple time and then asked, "Peter, are you from around here?"

"I'm from near here," I said defensively. "I grew up in Duluth."

"Pasties come with ketchup, unless you're from Mars or something." She eyed me suspiciously. "Well then, you're not Catholic or Lutheran. Are you a Methodist or one of those other offbeat religions?"

"Ketchup is fine," I said. Dottie nodded agreement as she jotted our order on a notepad.

"Pretty quiet for a Thursday night," Jenny said, looking around at the half-full dining area. There were a dozen gray-haired men at the bar. Two women sat at a table drinking umbrella drinks.

"I think all their business is dying off. Most of the World War II vets are either dead or unable to drive and the Viet Nam vets never got into the Legion the way the guys from the earlier wars did."

Norm, the bartender, came over with our beers and oak box tucked under his arm. A Viet Nam vet, his graying hair tied in a ponytail, Norm was a retired cabinetmaker who tended bar on the weekends "to get out of the house." He set the beers down and handed me the box.

"Not tonight, Norm," I said. I pulled out my wallet and pulled out a fifty-dollar bill, handing the box and the money back to him. "Thanks."

"Cigars?" Jenny asked as Norm slipped the money into the front pocket of his jeans.

Norm's face broke into a big smile and he released the brass latch on the box. The lid opened and on a field of green felt were a dozen military insignia and medals. He held them out proudly.

Jenny looked at them and asked, "Whose are they?"

Norm looked surprised. "Pete asked me to build a box for him. I went down to the woodworking shop by the old train depot and came up with a design and found some clear oak that looked like it needed a nice home."

I felt the crimson climbing my neck. I was at a loss for words. The box held pieces of my past that had been jammed in the back of a drawer in the misbegotten hope that having them out of sight would keep them out of mind and out of my dreams. Norm had shown me a box that he'd built for one of the other Iraq vets and I decided that it was time to bring everything into the light. But I wasn't ready to share them with Jenny.

150

Jenny took the box from Norm and ran her hand over the wood. "You did a lovely job, Norm," she said as he beamed with pride. She looked at me and pointed to a Silver Star that hung from a red, white and blue ribbon. "What's this?" she asked.

"It's a Silver Star," I replied.

"It's awarded for bravery beyond the call of duty," Norm explained when I didn't immediately respond.

Jenny's expression changed from curious to sudden comprehension. "Thanks, Norm," she said, dismissing him and pulling the oak box in front of her.

"Jeremy said that you threw him to the floor when Dolores was shooting at the rabbits. He said you reacted so fast that he didn't know what was going on."

"I wasn't sure what was happening," I said, not sure about the sudden change in topic, "so I decided that the best place for him was on the floor."

"It sounded like pure instinct to me."

"It was more self-preservation."

"Jeremy said you threw your body on top of him," Jenny replied. "That's not *self* preservation."

"I guess."

"You've never spoken about what you did in the Navy, Peter."

"No, I haven't."

"What did you do in the Navy?"

When I didn't respond, Jenny gave a hand wave indicating she wanted more information. "I was a Navy corpsman," I finally said.

"Like dispensing meds on a ship and treating sore throats?"

"More like an Army medic, only assigned to a Marine Corps platoon."

Dottie arrived with our pasties and set them down with silverware wrapped in paper napkins. Without words she made a point by taking a bottle of ketchup from a nearby table and setting it in front of me.

Jenny unwrapped her silverware and spread the napkin on her lap. She cut into her pasty releasing a puff of steam, then set her fork down and stared at me. "You were in Iraq? In combat? Is that why you have nightmares?"

"It's hard to say where the dreams come from. I have a lot of math anxiety and I sometimes dream about missing a math test."

Jenny ignored my flippant answer and touched the gleaming Purple Heart pinned in the box. She put her hand on my arm and looked into my eyes. "You were wounded? I've never seen any scars."

"Guys lost legs and worse. My little nick hardly counts."

"Where, Peter?"

I pointed to my left armpit. "A little piece of shrapnel from a roadside bomb caught me inside my arm. It was nothing more than a scratch."

"How many stitches did they put in your scratch?"

"It doesn't matter. The guys who don't come home and the ones who lose limbs are the ones who deserve Purple Hearts, not guys like me who never missed a day of duty. I felt like a fraud when they pinned it on me."

"What are these other medals that you haven't told me about?" she asked, pointing to the other ribbons and medals in the box.

"Jenny, I did a job there. It was a dirty, disturbing job with chaos raining around me at times. I did exactly what I was trained to do for people who depended on me to be there when they needed me."

"Do they give out Bronze Stars for competency?" she asked, pointing to the star suspended from a ribbon with two wide red stripes and narrow blue and white stripes in the center.

I could feel the color rise in my neck and approach my ears.

"You're embarrassed because you were brave and got medals?"

I dug into my pasty and pushed it around in the ketchup while I tried to come up with an answer. "Yes, I'm embarrassed for getting medals. I did what I was trained to do, nothing more, and someone thought I should have a couple of medals for that."

"Did it involve running out into scary places where people were shooting at you to drag wounded Marines to safety?"

"There's nothing heroic about it. I was scared shitless, but there were marines who might've died if I hadn't done what I'd been trained to do." I paused. "Can we end this discussion now?"

Jenny put her elbows on the table and cupped her chin in her hands. "All right, but which of these are for heroism?"

"The Bronze Star and the Silver Star."

"You did it twice?" she asked.

"I told you, it was my job. I didn't do it for the medals. I did it to save lives."

"Why haven't you ever told me about Iraq?"

"I spend most of my time trying to forget. It's not really dinner-table conversation."

"How bad was it?"

"It's not dinner-table conversation." I repeated. "Can we move to a different topic?"

"You have more medical training than I have. Why didn't you go to med school or to a physician's assistant program when you got back?"

"I'd simply had enough. I needed to move on."

"But you're wasting your training."

"Wasting what? I can't look at a rare steak without a flashback."

"OK. I'm beginning to understand now. The dreams that make you jump up in the middle of the night are flashbacks. Have you been diagnosed with PTSD?"

I pushed the pasty through some more ketchup and stared at the plate, knowing that I couldn't get a white lie past her. "I haven't had a clinical diagnosis of PTSD, but I suppose that would fit my symptoms."

"Music is your therapy," she said with newly understood conviction.

"Music is therapeutic and dealing with the residents lets me continue to help people."

"But you could be so much more."

I took her hand, "You put some texture in my life that make the days easier to take. I still have a lot of baggage to sort out before I'll feel whole again. Help me ease through it. OK?"

We spent the next few minutes in silence with Jenny apparently mulling over our discussion.

Trying to restart the conversation in a different direction I said, "Your mother warned me not to hurt Jeremy when I picked him up."

"Why on earth would she think that you'd hurt Jeremy?"

"She was concerned about him emotionally, not physically."

"It's interesting that she's concerned about you hurting Jeremy, but I'm sure she never mentioned me." She paused. "I'm sure she sees the same thing that I do whenever Jeremy talks about you. He idolizes you."

"He ignores me," I replied. "The first thing he does when he comes over is dig out the remote and turn on the television. The only time I seem to matter is when I'm feeding him. Which reminds me, he hid the remote and I've had to get off the couch to change television channels or to lower the volume since he was over."

"I overheard him telling his friend Jack what you did when the gunfire broke out. He made it sound like you were a hero." Jenny paused, then added, "The way he told it, there were bullets flying everywhere and you jumped up and rushed Dolores, taking the gun from her hand."

"First of all, we were only in danger because Dolores' eyesight is so poor. The only one who was safe was the stupid rabbit she was aiming at. Secondly, I didn't rush Dolores. I snuck along the side of her house and crept onto the porch. Thirdly, I didn't wrest the gun from her hand, but rather asked her to give it to me, and she handed it over."

"Jeremy's version is much more colorful. He told my mother. She was apoplectic about her only grandson being put in harm's way. I think Jeremy was reveling in her rant."

"I'm not sure what we should do with all of Dolores's guns," I said. "As long as I have the key to her gun cabinet, they're safe from her. But the gun cabinet is hardly burglar-proof, and I'm certain that some of those guns should be in a museum."

"Luckily, there isn't much burglary in Two Harbors," Jenny said as she considered the rest of her pasty. Her rate of consumption had dropped quickly once she reached the halfway point. She pushed the plate away. "But there are some predatory people around, and if word ever leaked out about her stash of collector's guns, they might disappear in the dark of the night."

"They'd have to get past Dolores," I said with a smile. "She may be old, but she's certainly not feeble."

"Dolores may be capable of independent living now, but one push and she has a broken hip that leaves her in a wheelchair if she doesn't die from pneumonia first."

"Maybe the Duluth train museum would like them for an exhibit. If there is some way to authenticate the Bowie pistol, it could be quite a tourist attraction."

We finished up and were ready to pay our bill when Dottie returned with her order pad.

"I think we're ready for our check," I said.

Dottie shook her head. "Didn't you notice the sign? We have Betty's Pies tonight. What flavor pie would you like? I recommend the gooseberry. You can get it with or without the ala mode."

"But..."

"But you'd rather have the blueberry? Is that it?" Dottie asked, closing the door on further discussion of skipping dessert.

"Gooseberry sounds good to me, but no ala mode," I said

"Same for me," Jenny said.

Chapter 21

Hugo's Bar is a dozen or so miles west of Two Harbors and the combination of the conversation, the pasty, beer. and pie was starting to feel like a bowling ball in my gut as we crossed over Boomer's Road. Boomer had been a colorful WWII pilot who returned to Two Harbors after the war and decided that he could break the sound barrier, creating a sonic boom by flying his Piper Cub in steep dives over town. No one ever heard the boom, but the nickname stuck, and the road he lived on was renamed.

Hugo's gravel parking lot was filled with cars and pick-ups when we arrived, and we had to park on some dead grass next to a small white building. Hugo's was a hodgepodge of additions tacked onto the old bar. The siding was weathered wood, and the smell of burgers cooking emanated from the rearmost addition. A walk-in cooler protruded from its side like a giant white ice cube. In the back parking lot were several small white buildings, each big enough for a single bed and a footlocker. They had been rental housing for transients who worked on the railroad in the heyday of the mining industry.

I could feel the amplified electric bass vibrating in my chest when I stepped out of the car, and as we rounded the corner to the front door I could hear Wendy's smoky alto voice singing the band's rendition of "Crazy."

Jenny and I had met two years ago when attending a wedding reception at Hugo's. At that time, the combination of smokers and poor ventilation left a blue haze hanging just below the ceiling that drove both of us out to the fresh air where we'd talked the evening away sitting on the back steps. I was pleased that Minnesota had enacted a smoking ban, meaning that the smokers were now gathered outside the doors instead of puffing away at their tables. What hadn't changed at Hugo's was the wall-to-wall and elbow-to-elbow crowd that jammed the place even on a weeknight. Wendy's band, The Gin Fizzes, wrapped up "Crazy" and announced a 15-minute intermission. With the smokers rushing for the doors, Jenny and I were able to grab a table about 20 feet from the right edge of the stage.

Jenny tried to tell me something but the cacophony of voices and clattering chairs made conversation impossible. I scanned the crowd and noted that none of our residents were in attendance. I'm sure that many of them would've enjoyed the outing, but driving after dark was not an option for most of them.

A slender blonde waitress, whom I recognized as Sheila, the owner's wife, came to the table and pecked my cheek. She was wearing a black t-shirt with Hugo's logo on the front, and a camo baseball cap. "When are you coming back to play another acoustic guitar night?" she asked. "The last one was a blast."

"I thought your crowds enjoyed livelier music than the songs I played."

Sheila shrugged. "The crowds change. Most are happy to hear any music at all."

"I can come up anytime you and Tony want me," I replied, almost yelling.

She nodded her understanding and replied, "I'll talk to Tony. He'll give you a call."

She took our order for two Summit beers. Because of the background noise I wasn't sure that she'd heard my order, so I hoped for the best as she threaded her way through the crowd back to the bar, stopping at another table for an order and swatting away the hand of a guy who tried to feel her butt.

"You made it!" Wendy yelled, cruising across the room.

She pulled a chair from the table beside us and flopped down as if she was exhausted. I'd never seen Wendy dressed in anything but business casual, which usually consisted of khaki slacks and a sweater or blouse. She was wearing a white seersucker dress with a peasant neckline. A little bear tattoo was peeking over the scoop of her blouse and it caught my eye, partly because of the location and partly because Wendy didn't strike me as a tattoo-type of person.

"Do you like Teddy?" Wendy asked, catching me gawking. I felt the red creeping up my neck again.

"Um, he's cute."

"And very discreet," Jenny added. "He isn't visible under the sweaters you wear at work."

"You can't see much of him," Wendy said, pulling at the elastic neckline until a small bowtie showed. "I think that his bowtie and belt are cute."

The bowtie was already on "untanned" skin, and I was apprehensive about the belt and anything below the bear's beltline. Luckily, Wendy stopped at the edge of her bra, which covered a corner of the bowtie, and gave me a wink.

"Had you worried, didn't I?" She said, obviously reveling in my discomfort. "I have a dolphin..."

"In a location we don't need to see," Jenny said, completing the sentence.

Sheila worked her way back through the crowd and set two Samuel Adams Summer Ales in front of us. "Tony says the last Friday in May is open if that works for you. The beers are seven bucks."

Sam Adams was hardly Summit, but it had taken her over ten minutes to get to the bar and back, and it was beer. I gave her ten dollars. "I'll check the calendar for May. Keep the change, and bring us two more when you get a chance."

She looked at the crowd. "It'll be awhile," she said as she disappeared into the milieu.

The drummer mounted the small stage and started tapping out a beat on the rim of the snare drum. The bassist quickly followed, playing a bass riff to the beat of the drum.

Wendy stood up. "Time for the next set," she said. "Are you guys going to stay around for a while?"

"I thought we would," I replied. "How long are your sets?"

"It varies. Most are about forty-five minutes. If you hang around, I'll let you buy me a beer at the next break," Wendy said before she wound her way through the crowd to the stage.

The band consisted of Wendy, as the lead singer, a guitarist, a bassist, the drummer, and a very talented woman who switched between mandolin, banjo, and violin. They played a mixture of light rock, country, and R&B that delighted the crowd. Wendy's sultry alto voice melded beautifully with the guitarist's tenor voice and when they sang "I Got You Babe, "the crowd was rocking.

With the break close at hand, and a couple of beers starting to back up in my bladder, I decided to make a bathroom run before the rush. I threaded my way through the tables, then pressed through the standing-room-only crowd to get in line at the men's room. A corkboard between the bathrooms hosted dozens of "For Sale" items, ranging from ATVs to guns and chainsaws. A single white sheet caught my eye. It read, "Lost Air Guitar $100 reward." The bottom edge of the sheet was a string of tabs with the phone number of the owner. It took me a second to catch the humor.

The bathroom rush came before I got out of the men's room, and rather than fight my way back to the table against the tide, I decided to walk around the outside of the building. There was an old outhouse behind the building and a group of young men gathered nearby under the mercury parking lot light. As I got closer I could see that they were throwing narrow knives at a piece of wood about eight inches square, and they were remarkably consistent at hitting the wood at ten or fifteen paces. I watched for a few minutes until one of the guys missed the board, apparently eliminating him from the competition. He came to the back of the crowd where I was standing.

"Is that some kind of throwing knife?" I asked the 20-something man. "Nothing special," he said, turning the double-edged, stiletto-like knife in his hand. "It's just a puku. Lots of us Finns carry them."

I flashed back to the small hole in Axel's shirt and Len's words that a narrow, double-edged knife had inflicted the deadly wound. I made a mental note to tell Len about the Finnish pukus, then I quickly ran the resident list through my head and came up with about fifteen Finnish names. Stella Ahonen's Finnish birthday party added another 30 or more Finns to the visitor's list that day. I sighed.

"Thanks," I said to the young man and went back into the bar.

"Was there a long line?" Jenny asked after I threaded my way through the shoulder-to-shoulder crowd back to the table. Wendy was sitting at the end of our table, but was chatting up a cute guy at the next table. She showed him a little more of her bear tattoo than we'd seen, generating a lecherous comment and something whispered in Wendy's ear. Wendy took a furtive glance at his left hand and noticed a tan line on his ring finger.

"Nice try, married boy," Wendy said before pulling her chair back to the end of our table. "Isn't that the way it goes; the nice ones are either married or gay," she said, sighing.

"I thought you liked the bass player," Jenny said.

Wendy shook her head, looking across the room to where the bassist was chatting up a 50-something woman who was trying to look like she was 30-something. "He's into cougars."

"Cougars?" I asked.

Wendy rolled her eyes. "You ought to get out more, Peter. Cougars are middle-aged women looking for younger men. Larry says he likes them because they're not hung up about casual sex, not worried about getting pregnant, and they tend to pay for everything. Being a boy toy works pretty well for him. I can't support him in the manner to which he's become accustomed.

"Joey, the guitar player, is more into women his own age," she said, pointing him out at the bar where he was hanging on a pretty young thing who was wearing a tank top that showed a large portion of a scaly dragon tattoo with its tail wrapped around her neck. "He's into the girl with the dragon tattoo tonight."

"I wonder if she wears a turtleneck to job interviews?" Jenny asked rhetorically.

"I think she's a massage therapist," I said, garnering inquisitive looks from both women. "I heard some guy at the bar say she rubbed him the wrong way."

Wendy moaned and Jenny punched my arm and said, "That's so lame."

The violinist and guitar player were back on stage. They started their own version of dueling banjos. Wendy jumped up from her chair as the rest of the band pressed their way through the crowd.

"They're actually very good," Jenny yelled to me over all the noise.

"They all were professionals in other places and decided to move back to the region after they didn't hit it big," I said. "Wendy told me that the violinist was first chair for the Knoxville, Tennessee, symphony, but missed the winters and her family. The bass player was with a couple of touring shows, and the guitar player toured with Steve Martin when he was doing his bluegrass thing."

Jenny leaned across the table and held my hand. "Your voice is as good as the guy playing guitar. If you practiced a little you could master the riffs he's playing and you could move beyond Friday nights at Hugo's bar and entertaining little old ladies."

I kissed her. "If I did, I could run off to Nashville or New York and play back-up occasionally while I waited tables. Then, a few years later, I would get fed up, come back here, and marry you."

Jenny's head jerked up. "Did you just propose to me?"

My jaw locked. I could see she was a little tipsy, but not so drunk she wouldn't remember this conversation in the morning. "It was kind of hypothetical. If all those things happened, would you still have me, was what I was saying, or asking." As the words tumbled out, they sounded lame even to me.

"So, you didn't propose?"

"When I propose, I will get on one knee and ask you in a very romantic way. It won't be in a noisy bar with cougars and dragon ladies when we've both been drinking."

"So, you're *going* to ask me to marry you?" she said in an outdoor voice.

"Can we have this conversation later?" I said into her ear.

"Maybe I won't say yes if you ask me later. I'd say yes if you ask me now."

It occurred to me, as she slurred her words, that I was getting her unfiltered feelings. There were only two possible ways to end the conversation: Plan A would get a "yes" answer and would be permanent. Plan B would be immediately messy and might mean that there might not ever be a chance to have a Plan A at some later time. There had to be a plan C. As it turned out, Wendy came to the rescue.

A round of applause rolled through the club as the last notes of "Blue Eyes Crying In The Rain" echoed through the rafters. Wendy stepped up to the microphone and said, "One of my close friends is a very talented musician, and he's in the audience tonight. If you encourage him with a round of applause, he might come up here and sing the Willy Nelson part of "Pancho and Lefty."

I was swept to the stage before I could say anything else to Jenny. After getting a loaner guitar and stumbling through a few bars, I became one with the band, and it was magical. Larry, the bass player, had a beautiful resonant baritone voice with just enough rasp to sound like Waylon

Jennings. I pulled off a pretty good Willy Nelson, and when the song ended, the club erupted.

The band kept me onstage for two more numbers, then Wendy told me they were going to wrap up with a Jackson Browne rendition of "Stay." "You're doing the falsetto verse," she whispered.

"I can't," I protested. "I've never done falsetto in front of an audience."

"You do it all the time in front of the residents."

"But half of them are deaf, and the other half would be happy to listen to a one-armed accordionist."

"Try."

When I hit the falsetto, "Oh won't you stay, just a little bit longer," the crowd cheered and whistled, and I floated through it on adrenaline. My voice held up, and the band picked up the rest of the vocals. When the applause stopped, people swarmed the stage and all the musicians were getting kudos. I was slapped on the back, knuckle-bumped, and kissed as I pressed my way through the crowd. A middle-aged woman with platinum blonde hair, who smelled like cigarettes, pressed herself against me and gave me a kiss that involved her tongue trying to find my tonsils. I pushed myself away, leaving her with a sad pout that made me believe I could've spent the night with my first cougar groupie. I felt a sudden urgency to find Jenny, hoping I hadn't contracted any communicable disease from cougar slobber.

I finally saw Jenny near the door talking to a man with hints of gray at his temples. Behind them was a tin sign advertising Katie's ice fishing school. It said that Katie would teach you how to keep your tip up. Tony, the owner, who sported a black goatee and his own camo cap, gave me a nod and asked, "Will that Friday work for you, Pete?"

"I'll check," I yelled over the crowd noise. He nodded and gave me a wave, then went back to filling the orders for the people still lined two-deep at the bar.

Jenny's expression was too serious for the venue and I wondered what was going on. When I got close she waved me over.

"Peter, this is Axel's son, Gary," Jenny said, trying to be heard over the crowd.

"I should've talked to you guys about the funeral a few days ago," he said apologetically. We leaned close to hear his soft voice. "I was hoping that we could add a military honor guard to the graveside service."

The adrenaline was still flowing and it took me a few seconds to get back to my "other" world. "Um, it's already Wednesday night and the funeral is Friday. I don't have much chance to set that up. If I'd had a couple more days, I might've been able to contact the American Legion or the VFW, but I'm pretty sure they couldn't get someone with this short notice."

"I'm sorry. My sister was supposed to tell you about dad's wishes for a military funeral, but I think she was more interested in spending his money to spite him. He was quite emphatic that he wanted to be cremated and buried with military honors. I didn't find out until this afternoon that she'd given you other directions." He spoke softly and I struggled to hear, almost putting my ear next to his lips.

"How did you find us here?" I asked.

"I called Whistling Pines and they told me that some-one named Wendy is an entertainer and almost everyone knew that you were going to see her perform tonight." He paused and shook his head. "I made some calls Monday, after dad died. I thought I might be able to get someone from the military to step up, but I haven't heard back from them."

"I just don't think I can pull it off," I said, looking at my watch.

Gary looked at his shoes and shook his head. "Were you at least able to find bagpipes?"

"We might have someone coming," I said, although Jenny was shaking her head. "But I'm not optimistic."

Gary was near tears. "I should've been on this yesterday. It's not your fault." He took a deep breath and shook his head. "I guess I'll call the consulate again and hope for the best." He shook our hands and turned away. I was pretty sure I'd just met Axel's one child who didn't make the list of probable killers.

As we walked to the car Jenny asked me, "Did he say he was calling the counselor or consulate?"

"I couldn't hear half of what he said. My ears are still ringing from the loud music."

I opened Jenny's car door and she turned to face me, planting a big kiss on my lips. "I know you had plans for tonight, but all this talk about the funeral has really squashed my libido. Do you think we could go back to your place and just snuggle? I just need you to hold me close tonight."

In this one case, the answer was clear. "Snuggling would be great."

Chapter 22

We held hands on the drive back to Two Harbors, then Jenny leaned back with her eyes closed. *"I've never heard you* perform most of the songs you played with the band tonight," Jenny said. "But you played like you'd practiced them a lot. How can you do that?"

"I play by ear," I replied. "I've heard the songs, so I recognize the background guitar chord progression. It's not that hard."

"You played a guitar riff the same as Jackson Browne plays on piano. That's not chords on a background guitar, and I'm sure it's not easy."

I struggled to find an answer. "There was a lot of downtime in Iraq, so I spent a lot of hours picking at my guitar. The Marines asked me to play a lot of their favorite songs, so I learned to stumble my way through any song they requested."

"You could be professional," Jenny said, taking my hand and squeezing it. "I'm just lucky you've chosen to be here with me."

Within two miles her hand relaxed and she was making soft sleepy sounds. I still had enough adrenaline from the performance to fuel a 747. Visions of the bright lights of Nashville and Memphis with huge venues full of cheering fans flowed through my head. Pretty women with skimpy costumes were throwing underwear and hotel keys on the stage. Then I flashed ahead to the generic motels with little bottles of shampoo and crappy fast food and thousands of miles in crowded tour buses. The highs from the concerts would give way to lows of the hours hanging around hotels and arenas waiting, and waiting.

My life now was quiet and regular. There weren't many high highs, but the lows weren't very low. People showed appreciation for what I did every day. The residents loved me and my music. Better than that, there was Jenny, who wanted to marry me and be with me the rest of my life. I had a sudden flashback to Hugo's and the drunk woman who slipped me her tongue and I knew that I didn't want a life on the road, especially if it involved drunk middle-aged groupies who smelled of Marlboros and stuck their tongues in my mouth.

The rumble of the tires on the gravel gave way to the whine of asphalt. As we neared Two Harbors a billboard advertising two-thousand-square-foot lakeside timeshares with mini-bars and whirlpool tubs loomed next to the road. Ironically, we were passing old tourist cabins that had been built in the 1930s when tourists were able to drive two-lane Highway 61 from the Twin Cities to Two Harbors in four hours, happy to rent a cabin with a bed and a nearby out-house. People's expectations of their vacation rentals had changed during the past century. My life was somewhere in between, with an expectation of indoor plumbing, but not a hot tub. Iraq helped me realize what was important and I was happy to exchange a high-stress life for Whistling Pines and Jenny.

The adrenaline had worn off by the time we reached my neighborhood. Jenny had been asleep for most of an hour. Her eyes opened as I turned onto the side streets. She looked out the side window and watched the houses pass as I wound down the street to my house.

"Peter, are you prepared for the funeral?" she asked sleepily.

"I think so. I mean, there will be a funeral. We have a church and minister. Wendy has the music under control; at least she told me that she has plans and she's never let me down. The bus is coming to deliver the residents to the church, and I spoke with the head of the Ladies Aide Society, and they will have lunch for two hundred people. So, I think everything is prepared."

"What about the bagpipes?"

"I don't know."

"Are you going to call the VFW and American Legion?"

"There isn't any point. It's too late for them to pull together an honor guard."

"Will it go smoothly?"

"I have no idea. If it doesn't, the funeral will be memorable."

We walked hand-in-hand to the house in silence. Jenny stripped off her coat and hung it on a peg by the door. She looked troubled.

"*I feel bad*," she said. "There will be a hundred or more people at the funeral, and I don't think that one of them will be there for anything but the spectacle. I mean, no one will be there because Axel was their friend or because they respected him. They're all coming to see the bagpipes or for the lunch."

"*Funerals aren't for the dead;* they're for the living. Hardly anyone comes for the deceased. I*'ve* talked to our residents on the way back from the funerals and do you know what they talk about? They talk about what was served for lunch, or how good or bad the dead person looked, or how many of their old friends they saw. It's a social event, like an extended family reunion. People come from all over to see each other. All that will happen Friday."

When we climbed into bed, Jenny in an oversized purple Vikings jersey, and me in boxers, Jenny seemed subdued. She turned her back to me and pulled my arm across her waist and wiggled until we were nested like spoons.

"I want people to come to my funeral because they like me," she said after a moment of silence.

"I'm sure people will come because they like and respect you," I said, pulling her tighter and kissing her neck.

She rolled over, so we were face-to-face, and she slid her finger down my jaw. "You were really good with the band tonight."

"I was scared when Wendy asked me to sing falsetto."

"I wish I'd had a video camera. The expression on your face was priceless." She pressed her face to mine and kissed me gently. "I can't sleep."

"Oh?"

"I shaved my legs this morning."

"That's nice," I said, not quite knowing where the discussion was going. "They're nice and smooth."

"Peter, can you take a hint?"

"Um...I think so. Why?"

"That was a hint."

"The shaved legs, you mean?"

"Uh huh," she replied, pressing her hips against my pelvis. "It feels like you're catching on."

"I think I've got the idea now."

Chapter 23

Thursday

I didn't sleep well with the combination of adrenaline, loud music, rich food, passion, and a few too many adult beverages. At 3:00 AM I gave up on the prospect of sleep, slipped into the shower and let the water pound on my neck and back until the hot water turned icy. I did a quick shampoo in cold water and came out of the shower chilled and wide awake. I quietly found a golf shirt and khaki pants in the closet, and socks and underwear folded in a laundry basket on top of the washer. I slipped them on downstairs. I didn't want to wake Jenny so I decided to forego breakfast rather than rattle around the kitchen making coffee and trying to find something edible. In the kitchen, I found the display box with the medals sitting on the table. I gently lifted the lid, looked at the ribbons and immediately felt sad. I made a spot in the cupboard next to the cereal and slipped the box out of sight. I left Jenny a note and considered locking the door for her safety, but I couldn't remember where the key might be. I hadn't locked it since I moved in. There never seemed to be a need before. I thought about hiring a locksmith, then decided I was being needlessly paranoid.

The Thursday morning newspaper was on the door-step when I walked out. I quickly scanned the headlines and found that Axel's murder had slipped from the page 1 headline to page 4. The article identified Axel as the previously unnamed murder victim and said the medical examiner determined the cause of death to be a stab wound. The reporter quoted a BCA investigator who thought a suspect would be in custody within a few days.

"I wonder if the medical examiner found a heart when he looked inside Axel's chest?" I muttered.

The whole milieu of the previous evening had my mind swimming — Wendy's craziness, the band's pounding rhythms, Jenny's unveiled hint that she wanted a marriage proposal, and unanswered questions about Axel's death and whoever hated him enough to kill him. And, of course, the funeral plans. There were so many motives for some-one to kill Axel and dozens of people who hated him; my mind boggled with the combinations of motive and oppor-tunity.

As I drove through the dark streets of Segog I tried to sort the tidbits I'd gathered into some sort of organized pat-tern. The whole thing was becoming a kaleidoscope with changing patterns and colors as I twisted the information in my mind. I was overwhelmed by the irregular spurts of information that came to me from so many disconnected sources. When I'd taken a criminology course, they'd said to organize a timeline of events and then use that to elimi-nate and prioritize suspects. What they hadn't told me was that there could be a dozen or more suspects, with motives that were spread over decades, and that the information would pop up unexpectedly when I wasn't prepared to receive it or deal with it. I was tempted to give up my role as undercover investigator, throw the whole thing back to Len Rentz, and go back to being a pretty good activities director.

The pre-dawn calm lent an air of eeriness to the Whistling Pines parking lot. I shivered as I walked across the open expanse of the employee parking lot behind the building. I could hear the gurgling wash of gentle Lake Superior swells as they struck riprap along the shoreline and receded. Any other morning I might've been tempted to walk to the edge of the lawn and look at the lake in the moonlight, but Axel's murder left me unsettled.

I could smell coffee as I slipped in the delivery door. I quickly shed my coat in my office before returning to the kitchen for a caffeine fix. There were already a half dozen women in the kitchen. Two huge stainless steel stockpots were already bubbling with soup and three women chatted as they chopped vegetables and slid them into broth. Two other women were pulling dough from the paddles of a Hobart mixer, and a third was preparing pans for caramel rolls that would soon be baking.

They were all in their own worlds as they chatted over their chores and no one seemed to notice as I tapped a cup of coffee from the urn and wandered into the dining room. A lone figure was carefully spreading white tablecloths on the tables, then setting each with water glasses and stainless flatware. I watched silently as Florie smoothed the wrinkles from the tablecloths and arranged them carefully before putting out the place settings. As she shook out a folded tablecloth, Florie saw me watching her and smiled.

"Peter, are you staring at my behind again?" she asked.

I could feel the red creeping up my face. "I was just thinking about how efficient you were, and what great pride you take in your work," I replied.

Florie was working at Whistling Pines when I started two years ago, and considering that her skin was the color of dark mocha in a land of blue-eyed blondes, she had a way of becoming part of the wallpaper when she chose to be invisible. She worked the same 5AM shift as the early kitchen staff where she prepped the dining room while the cooks started dough and soups, and went home shortly after the lunch tables were cleared and reset for dinner. She finished arranging the tablecloth and swayed across the room. She picked up a coffee cup, filled it, then sat down in a chair at the nearest table. She patted the chair next to her and I sat down, even though the narrow distance between our chairs violated my Minnesota sense of personal space.

"I hear that you're the police spy who's investigating that old bastard's death." Close-up I could see her face looked tired and her eyes were bloodshot.

I shifted in the chair, mostly because I wasn't comfortable being characterized as a spy. "I've been asking around a little." Then I paused and the rest of her words struck me. "Why did you call him an old bastard?"

Florie smiled and leaned closer to me in a way that made her more-than-ample girth strain against the buttons of her dress. Without thinking, my eyes wandered to the Grand Canyon of cleavage as she said, "I called him a bastard because that is the technical description of someone who was born out of wedlock."

"What?" Startled, my eyes met hers again.

"Peter, honey, old Axel was a bastard in the literal sense of the word, as were at least two of his children." Florie had a smile that disarmed me to the point where I felt like I was talking with my own minister, or maybe my grandmother. I felt like I'd known of her for most of my life, and when I first met her I thought she was old. As time passed, she seemed to get younger, and now I was guessing that she wasn't much more than 50 years old, but her eyes looked like they'd seen a century of experience.

Florie scooped up our coffee cups and headed for the kitchen, leaving me stunned by her words. When she came back her gait made her body glide with the rhythm of her steps. She noticed the way I was watching her and as she set the steaming coffee cups on the table she leaned close and wiped something from my cheek in a way that was both maternal and sensuous at the same time.

"Peter, I see that you have come to appreciate the beauty of a full-figured woman." She did a pirouette and then sat in the chair, again violating my personal space. "I don't know what you see in the little strawberry blonde girl that you chase around. She hasn't seen enough of the world to know what's real and what's not, and she's so skinny that you probably cut yourself on those sharp little bony hips of hers."

The red started rising at my neck again. I prepared to make a witty retort but had been masterfully diverted from my previous train of thought. Florie knew which buttons to push and had pushed all of mine in great style.

"How do you know about the parentage of Axel's children?"

Florie's eyes twinkled. "Honey, when I moved to this frozen hellhole from Georgia, Axel was the only person who'd give a black girl a job. I suspected that he thought he could bully me into being his personal servant, but he didn't know me very well, and he greatly underestimated my moral character and my willingness to tell all I knew to interested parties, like his wife."

"What did he hire you to do?"

"I was a waitress at his bar down in Mahtowa for a while, and then I managed his restaurant out on Fish Lake, west of Duluth, for a few years."

"That's quite a step up, moving from waitress to restaurant manager. You must've been very good."

"Of course I was very good, and I kept very good notes. I saw who was coming and going at the bar, and which guys were leaving with other people's wives. A few of them tried to hit on me, but I am quite capable of setting boundaries and defending them. After awhile they gave up, and then, when I'd drop a name or two, or ask where the previous night's conquest was, they caught on to the fact that I was paying too much attention to what was going on, and that they'd best stay on my good side for the sake of their marriages."

"So, you know where the skeletons are buried," I summarized. "And Axel moved you to Fish Lake to minimize the risk."

"I'd like to think that he saw how much more money he was making on the nights when I filled in as bartender, and saw how much calmer the crowd was when I worked, and decided that he needed someone to clean up the Fish Lake restaurant before it went bankrupt."

"Did you turn it around?"

Florie laughed. "I did! And it started making money. People started coming in because the food was good and I poured a fair drink. Pretty soon, it became a cash cow and Axel was making a mint off of it."

"I sense there is a catch here."

"The restaurant went from bankrupt to wealthy, and Axel seized the opportunity to sell it while he could show a buyer a great set of books."

"What happened to you, Florie?"

"The new owner put his daughter in as the new manager and hired her worthless, drug-dealing husband as the cook. I got fired."

"Axel didn't hire you back at the bar?"

"Oh, hell no! Like you said, I knew where too many skeletons were hidden and he saw that as a liability. I knew too much and he was too pleased that he'd stuck it to me. I think he was hoping I'd catch a bus back to Georgia."

"Why didn't you? You called this place a frozen hellhole. Why not go back?"

Florie's face clouded. "Some skeletons are scarier than others." Her face brightened and she added, "And I met a nice guy who thought a curvy dark-skinned girl with a sense of humor was a pretty good companion."

"I guess I've never asked about your family. Do you have any children?"

"I never married and I wasn't about to raise a bastard child by myself. I just kept looking for Mr. Right and made the most of the ones who were wrong while they were around. How about you, Peter? When are you going to make an honest woman of that skinny little girl? She thinks the world of you. I can see it in her eyes."

Again I felt the red creep up my neck.

"You're what? You're scared? You're taking advantage of a good thing. You're not into buying a cow when the milk is free. What?" Her face was mirthful, but the words were pointed. "Honey, you've got to get serious or turn that girl loose to find someone who'll spend the rest of his life with her."

Once again Florie had turned the conversation in another direction and I tried to steer it back again. "How did you end up here, at Whistling Pines?"

"A girl doesn't live on and love alone," she said, laughing at her own joke. "I get to socialize here, and the clientele are a lot better than the folks I was hanging around with at the bars."

"How did it go with Axel showing up as a resident?"

Florie nodded her head. "He didn't care if I was here or not. As far as he was concerned the world revolved around him and all the rest of us were just pawns he used to get to the top of the heap."

"He must've known that you were unhappy about getting fired at the restaurant."

"Oh, he knew that, honey. He was aware of my unhappiness because I told him in the most basic words I could find. You know what he did when I reamed him? He laughed. He leaned back in his old office chair and he laughed at me. He called me a stupid bitch and told me to get out before he called the cops."

"Did you hate him enough to kill him?"

Florie closed her eyes like she was replaying an old scene in her head. "Back then, if I'd had a gun, I'd have shot him. But you know what? He wasn't worth it. Besides, I got even, and the best part is that he never knew how."

"What fun is revenge if you don't see the target suffer?" I asked.

"His wife got some pictures in the mail that opened her eyes to some things that were going on. I'm pretty sure that his life went into the shitter for awhile because of me. I saw him suffer and squirm. He just never knew that it was me who was making the waves that he was rowing against."

"But, I thought his wife was a beaten woman who went along with anything Axel wanted?"

"Oh, that's what Axel wanted people to think. In reality, Enid was a cunning fox who had him by the balls. Let me tell you what she did." Florie leaned close. "They had a daughter, but she knew that he wanted a son to carry on the businesses and family name. Well, when she found out that he was sleeping around while she was pregnant, she went and got an abortion, and he lost the only son he might've ever had."

"How could you know something like that?"

"Axel got the mumps after the abortion and they went down on him. The doctors said his little swimmers were all dead and that he would be 'shooting blanks' the rest of his life. His wife had the two boys afterward and Axel was too vain to admit that he couldn't be their biological father."

"Wow! That's pretty heavy revenge," I said, thinking about the family dynamics and considering how much of the dysfunction might be explained if the family knew about all these skeletons.

"Peter, I'm going to tell you something very important." She took my hand in hers and looked deeply into my eyes. "There is more going on than you know about. Do you understand what I'm saying?"

"Not really," I replied. "I thought Axel's death had something to do with Whistling Pines."

"Honey, I think Axel's death is related to things that were set in motion long before Axel came here." Florie released my hand and stood up. "Now get out of here and pretend we never had this conversation."

As she walked away I pondered her words. Obviously she knew more than she'd said. Was she trying to throw me a red herring to get me off the track? Florie made it sound as if Axel had suffered plenty when she'd extracted her revenge and I had the impression she had little remaining motive to murder him.

Chapter 24

I headed back to my office wondering what had just happened. My mind drifted back to the conversation that Jenny and I had with my neighbor Dolores and her tales of intrigue, and people close to Axel being killed or disappearing. I was so deep in my thoughts that I didn't hear Len walk up behind me until he cleared his throat.

"Geez, Len, do you have to sneak up on me like that?"

"No sneaking involved, Peter," Len said as he fumbled with the pipe he'd fished from his breast pocket. "You weren't paying attention." He took out a chrome-plated tool and fiddled with the tobacco before putting the pipe between his lips. He pulled out a lighter and was about to fire up when I stopped him.

"You can't smoke inside, Len."

"I know," he said, making the pipe bob with each syllable. "That doesn't mean I can't get the oral pleasure of having it in my lips. You know, they say that sixty percent of the addiction is the smoking ritual, and the oral pleasure of stuffing something between your lips."

"That sounds a little kinky if you ask me."

"There's nothing sexual about it. As a matter of fact, people claim that it's more of a return to nursing like a baby."

"Either way, it seems like something that you should step away from."

"I'll make you a deal, Peter. You find the killer and I'll quit smoking again. Until then, leave me to my vices and tell me what you've heard."

"Florie Stevens used to work for Axel and she said that there are a lot of skeletons buried."

Len gave up the search for his lighter and put the pipe back between his lips as he pushed papers aside to sit in my guest chair. "Now that's a name that hasn't been on my radar before. I mean, I know who Florie is, but I've never had any reason to interact with her, which usually means that she's an upstanding citizen, or at least someone who spends her evenings at home not making noise with the folks who hang out at the bars. Where did you run into Florie?"

"She works the early shift in the kitchen here and was setting breakfast tables. We talked over a cup of coffee for a few minutes. She told me something else. Axel's two sons are not biologically his. She claims that his wife had them after he was no longer able to father a child."

Len froze. "Say that again."

"Axel caught the mumps after his daughter was born, and it did something to his testicles. When his wife learned about his philandering, she got even with him in a way that he couldn't protest publically. If he told anyone that he couldn't be the father of the boys, then everyone would know that he wasn't the stud that he claimed to be."

"Wow! That sure puts a crimp in the theory that the killer was one of the women that he'd scorned here."

"What women had he scorned here?" The question came from Jenny, who had apparently been listening outside the door.

"Good morning. One of our theories was that Axel had been having an affair with one of the women here, and that she killed him after he dumped her," I explained.

"First of all," Jenny said firmly, "the theory shouldn't contain the possessive pronoun "our," because you, Peter, are not investigating this crime. Secondly, there was no affair and hence no scorned woman. Thirdly, being impotent is not a barrier to sexual intimacy since the invention of the penile implant, and more recently, Viagra."

"You knew that Axel was sterile?" Len asked.

"That's immaterial. Most men his age suffer from either erectile dysfunction or low libido. The age of modern pharmaceuticals has made that irrelevant, and a little blue pill can do wonders for nearly anyone. Well, anyone it doesn't kill because their blood pressure drops."

"But," Len pointed his unlit pipe at Jenny. "The BCA didn't find any blue pills in the search of his apartment."

"There are HIPAA rules about patient privacy," Jenny replied.

"The patient is dead, Jenny," Len reminded her. "The only one who cares if Axel was using blue pills is me, and I only care because it affects my pool of potential murder suspects. I'd like to know about his partners."

"Well, then, I guess I'd better tell you before you tie me to a chair and turn a hot light on my head."

"Oooh," Wendy said, from somewhere outside the office door. "I love it when you talk dirty, like you're having phone sex. Does this involve handcuffs, too?"

"Darn it, Wendy," Jenny cursed as the color rose in her cheeks. "Why does everything have to be sexual with you?"

Wendy crowded into the office with the three of us, which left none of us with any personal space. Having been inside Humvees rolled by roadside IEDs in Iraq, I often feel a little claustrophobic in my cubbyhole office. The fourth person in the tiny space was too much for me to handle.

"All right!" I said, rising from my chair. "Everyone, get out of my office. I need some air."

"But I heard all the talk about the blue pills and the hot lights," Wendy said as we all retreated into the lobby. " I didn't know you had a cop in there with you, and Peter, I just came down to tell you that the Canadian bagpiper called me and her minivan broke down somewhere outside Kenora."

"What Canadian bagpiper? I haven't contacted any bag-pipers, much less any from Canada." I was almost shouting.

"Sure you have," Wendy said as she swept past me and fell into my desk chair. Her hands manipulated the computer mouse and within seconds my nightmare was being replayed to the tune of "Loch Lomond." There on the screen was the topless blonde, playing plaid bagpipes, and bouncing merrily as she belted out the tune. "See?"

As quickly as she appeared, the piper was gone, and my electronic in-box opened. Wendy quickly clicked open an e-mail and read it aloud. "Dear Peter, I'm responding to confirm your earlier e-mail. I am happy to drive to Two Harbors, Minnesota, to play the pipes for a funeral. I under-stand the family's wishes and your frustration in not finding a local piper, so I agree to waive my usual fee as long as you pay for my mileage and for two nights at the Holiday Inn next to the Mall of America. She signed it Laura Good."

Jenny was drilling holes in my head with her glare, and Len was suppressing a laugh but it finally broke through as a raspy coughing fit. Wendy jumped from my chair, and stepped behind Len, wrapping her arms around him, like a bear hug, and doing a Heimlich maneuver on him while he waved his pipe in the air. I knew that you shouldn't do a Heimlich on someone who was breathing, but Jenny grabbed my arm before I could intervene.

"How could you order a stripper for Axel's funeral?" Jenny asked, almost seething.

"I didn't! Someone is using my e-mail account. Besides, her e-mail doesn't say anything about stripping. It only says that she's coming to play the pipes."

"How naïve do you think I am, Peter? Did you look at her website?" Jenny rolled her eyes. "Of course you looked at her website. Why else would it be among the "Internet Favorite Websites" on your computer? What's the matter with you?"

I pulled free of Jenny's grasp and grabbed Wendy before she could Heimlich Len a third time. Len was turning purple from lack of air and I was afraid Wendy might've broken a couple of Len's ribs. Len bent over and drew a couple of deep breaths as we all waited silently. And then he started laughing.

"This is NOT funny!" Jenny said.

By the time he straightened up, tears were streaming down his face. "Oh, Jenny, if you could've seen your face when that girl popped up on the computer screen, you'd be laughing too." He reached out and gave her a fatherly hug.

Next he turned to Wendy. "Since you seem to be the one with Peter's computer password, would you care to tell us when you asked the stripper to drive down for the funeral?"

"Peter never turns his computer off, and he hasn't been using a password," Wendy countered. "It could've been anyone."

"It could've been, but it wasn't anyone. It was you. Correct?" Len asked.

Wendy looked at her shoes. "I suppose it could've been me. But there are other suspects you'll probably want to question."

"Did you give Peter's credit card out, too?"

"No way!" Wendy protested. "I'm sure he'd used it on some website that wasn't secure and it was scooped up by an Internet bot or someone who was phishing his computer."

"You're paying for a hooker to rent a motel at the Mall of America?" Jenny asked Wendy.

"It's every girl's dream shopping location," Wendy said. "People fly from all over, even Japan, for a weekend of shopping there. When we were negotiating, I suggested it, and Laura jumped right on it, offering to do the funeral for nothing if we paid for her mileage and motel."

"I find that hard to believe," Jenny said.

"Well, um, she did mention that there's a convention in Minneapolis and that she might be able to earn a little spending money. I think she meant that she was going to put out a tam-o-shanter and play her bagpipes in one of the skyways down by the convention center."

"I hate to say this," Len said, stuffing the pipe back in his pocket. "But I'm a cop, and I didn't hear that you arranged for a Canadian prostitute to drive to Minneapolis during a convention weekend so she could earn money to spend at the Mall of America."

Wendy looked anything but contrite. "She told Peter, or Peter's e-mail, that she'd even show him what pipers wear under their kilts."

The million-candlepower glare was back and I felt a pinch on my bicep. "That's one question that will remain a mystery to Peter," Jenny said.

"Ouch! I wasn't the one who asked. Why am I getting pinched?" I yelped.

Chapter 25

Miriam walked toward us wearing her food-stained apron, and asked, "Has anyone seen Florie? She was setting tables but no one has seen her for like fifteen minutes."

I pulled Len with me as I ran for the dining room's back door, the last place I'd seen Florie when I left the dining room. "Florie implied that she could be in danger by sharing information about Axel," I said over my shoulder as we jogged across the dining room. "I wonder if someone overheard us talking?"

The dining room opened onto a patio that overlooked a huge lawn leading to the cliffs above the town and a spectacular view of Lake Superior. A weather front had moved through and the warm damp air had dumped rain overnight. The cool ground caused eerie wisps of fog to form. Across the lawn was a stand of huge Norway pines that formed the north border of the grounds. Beyond the pines was a copse of poplar trees. I saw a bluish glow that looked like an LED flashlight and I took off running. I could hear Len start out close behind me, but he quickly faded, unable to keep up with my sprint.

In the morning twilight trees loomed in front of me and the faint light darted in and out of the trees. I dodged trees and rocks. Underbrush ripped at my pants. In my head-long dash to follow the light, I was completely blindsided by the blow that left me with a floating sensation before I fell to the ground.

My next recollection was chattering voices, stars spinning before my eyes, and a wave of nausea that forced me to purge the contents of my stomach onto my chest. I closed my eyes only to have an eyelid lifted and a blinding light flashed in and out of my eye.

"Peter, can you hear me?" Jenny asked.

"Get the light out of my eyes," I said, pushing the flashlight aside. I blinked my eyes a few times, but everything was blurry and had a rosy cast. "I was following a flashlight. Did you see the light?"

"What light, Peter?" Jenny asked.

"There was a light in the trees. Someone was running with a light."

"Peter," this time I heard Len's voice, "I found some rabbit snares set among the pines and some small footprints. I think one of the neighbor kids was checking his trap line and you probably saw his flashlight."

"Did he hit me with a baseball bat?"

"Actually, it looks like you ran headlong into a low pine branch," Len replied. "I was running after you, yelling for you to stop, and then you looked like something out of a Roadrunner cartoon. You hit the branch so hard that your feet lifted right off the ground."

The nausea eased enough to let the searing pain in my forehead leak through, and suddenly I felt like I'd been hit by, well, a tree. "Where's Florie?"

"She was taking a smoke break behind the dumpster," Jenny said.

I tried to push myself up to a sitting position, but was met with physical restraint from Jenny, and another wave of nausea. This time I turned my head and retched into the pine needle duff under the huge Norway pine that had clocked me. The wind moaned through the pine branches, giving me a sudden chill.

I felt Jenny dabbing at my forehead and each dab felt like I was being stabbed. "Will you stop that? It hurts."

"Sorry," Jenny said. "I was trying to mop up some of the blood. You were bleeding like a proverbial stuck pig for a while. I think you should go to the emergency room for few stitches."

"I've had worse head bangs than this. Just let me get back to my office," I said as I pushed myself from the ground. "I'll be fine if I sit for a while." That said, my world started moving and I had to grab Len's arm to stay upright.

It was embarrassing to have a herd of people helping me through the dining room door as the early-bird residents were shuffling in for breakfast. Every head turned to look at me and Howard Johnson stopped a few feet short of our group.

"Jenny," Howard said, "what in hell happened to Peter?"

"He had a little run-in with a low-hanging branch," she replied.

Chapter 26

When I returned to my office after lunch the phone was ringing, which elevated the dull ache in my head to a sharp pain. I scooped up the phone, as much to stop the noise as to answer the call. "This is Peter."

"Peter, this is Pastor Hamlin." My mind searched quickly for a connection, and I looked at the caller ID for help, *Two Hrbrs Luth.*

"Pastor, what can I do for you?" I said just as I realized that the pastor was the person who was conducting Axel's funeral. Anxiety swept over me.

"Actually, I think that I can help you," the pastor said, lightly. "Our secretary has been swamped with people calling to get the details of Axel Olson's funeral. She started counting yesterday and came to me when the tally surpassed the capacity of our sanctuary."

"Oh, Lord," I whispered to myself.

"That's exactly what I said, Peter. And the Lord answered my prayer. I spoke with my friend, John Pyne, the pastor at North Shore Lutheran Church, on London Road, in Duluth. They have a huge church that can easily accommodate the 300 to 400 people we think are coming. I took the liberty of asking him if we could move the funeral to his church and he was delighted to be of help."

"Four hundred people," I said to myself.

"I know! That's quite a turnout for a funeral. I'm not at all acquainted with Axel, or his family, but he must've been quite a figure in the community for so many people wanting to remember him."

"Oh yes, Pastor Hamlin, he was quite a figure in the community."

"Was he a war hero, too, Peter? Quite a few people have asked about the bagpipe honor guard."

I found myself at a loss for words. "Um, I can't really say." I had a sudden memory of the photo in the broken picture frame — Axel receiving a military decoration. Just as quickly the picture changed to 400 disappointed people expecting a bagpipe honor guard and, instead, getting Wendy playing "Loch Lomond" on the organ. Not to mention 400 people fighting over half enough food.

"Is something wrong? I thought you'd be happy that I was able to find a bigger church."

"It's very kind of you to help us out this way. It's just that I won't have the time or resources to notify all the people who are planning to attend."

"Peter, I've already anticipated your problem. I have the Ladies Aide Society coming in this afternoon. The ladies will call the family and all the people who've been making inquiries to let them know that we've moved the funeral to Duluth. I've even contacted the *Duluth News Tribune* and they'll have a corrected obituary in tomorrow's newspaper."

"Pastor," I said, at a loss for words.

"Really, Peter, no thanks are necessary. I'm happy to be of service to you and the family. Just let me know if there is anything else I can do."

I thought about asking him to find a piper, but decided that I shouldn't ask for any miracles beyond those that he was already providing. Instead, I just said, "Thanks."

Wendy was standing behind me when I hung up the phone. "Are you okay? I heard that you got a nasty bump on the head." When I turned so she could see the stained shirt and the darkening rings under my eyes, she recoiled.

"Not only do you look bad, but the blood on your shirt is a little distressing. Do you have an extra shirt?"

I looked at the front of my shirt, and then at my reflection in the computer screen. "This is becoming a bad day."

"I read your horoscope; it says that Libras should stay home and pull the covers over their heads."

I was having a hard time focusing and Wendy drifted in and out of my focal distance. "Can you hold still?"

"I'm not moving, Peter."

"Aw, crap."

Jenny showed up, also out of focus, and applied something that felt like it had come from the polar ice cap against my forehead. "If you refuse to go to the emergency room, this will at least minimize the swelling."

"If it doesn't give me a brain freeze," I said, trying to push her hand away, but I just didn't have the strength or resolve to fight her.

"You don't have to be a macho hero here, Peter," Jenny said, pressing the ice pack against my forehead. "You, of all people, know you could use a couple stitches in that gash in your forehead. Instead, you'll have to let me put a couple butterfly closures on your forehead and then put up with the scar."

"I don't have time to go to the hospital. There's too much left to do before the funeral. Can we move on?" I asked. "The funeral is being moved and we've got work to do."

"When did that happen?" Jenny asked as she opened a pack of sterile surgical butterflies and carefully applied several to my forehead.

"Pastor Hamlin called and they're moving the funeral to a bigger church on London Road in Duluth. He's having the Ladies Aide notify people of the change and there will be a revised obituary in the paper tomorrow."

"Cool!" Wendy blurted out.

"What?"

"That's really cool. They have this giant pipe organ that's got like ten octaves. I went to an organ recital for the University music department there. The organ is awesome and the acoustics in the sanctuary are more awesome. I can hardly wait to get my hands on it. I'll have to go down early tomorrow morning to practice."

I moaned. "Wendy, you have to call cousin Enos to let him know that he's driving the bus to Duluth instead of to the Two Harbors Lutheran Church."

"How about the Canadian hooker?" Len's voice came from around the corner. "Shouldn't someone contact her and let her know about the change?"

"Technically, she's got a phone sex site, so she's not a hooker," Wendy explained.

Len tilted his head down and looked over the top of his glasses at Wendy. "A phone sex operator wouldn't come to Minneapolis for a convention. She could take the calls in Winnipeg."

"Um, she's coming to the Mall of America for the shopping. I think the convention came up as a sidelight in all our e-mail correspondence."

"Guys, my head's about to break open and the pain is killing me," I complained. "Can you take your discussion outside?"

"Peter, you started to tell me about Florie's theories about Axel's murderer," Len said after Wendy left.

I started to shake my head, "no," before I realized that even a small motion caused me immense pain. "She didn't tell me that."

"Maybe she doesn't know that she knows the motive," Len said.

"Huh?"

"Florie knows about a whole bunch of Axel's dirty laundry, and she's been sharing pieces with you. She might have the piece that'll let us put the puzzle together." Len reached back and pulled the door shut. He patted his pockets until he found the lighter and lit the pipe as I watched silently. He inhaled deeply, closed his eyes, and then held his breath. An aura of satisfaction spread across his face. I didn't have the energy to stop him.

"She threw out like ten things. How do we find out which one is the motive?"

"Maybe she didn't tell you everything she knows," Len said as pipe smoke leaked from his mouth. "She may have exposed the tip of the iceberg to you, but there could be more that she didn't mention."

Something that Florie said hung in the back of my mind like it was hidden behind a black curtain. It suddenly popped to the surface. "Florie said something about Axel traveling around in his Lincoln. Did you ever check his car to see if there's anything in it that might point to the killer?"

"The BCA went over it with a fine-toothed comb. The agent who did the search said the outside looked like he'd been driving by Braille, but the inside was mostly clean," Len said.

"Driving by Braille?" I asked.

"Every fender was dented, like he'd been playing bumper cars," Len replied. "I doubt that he could even see the corners of the fenders of that big old Town Car."

The office door flew open and Wendy stood there glaring at us. "All right, this is not acceptable. You can't smoke in here. Besides, your pipe tobacco smells like you swept it off a barn floor."

I tried to protest, but Wendy cut me short as Len searched for a place to dump his pipe. "I don't care who was smoking, Peter. It's your office and you shouldn't allow it." She stood, with hands on hips, looking menacing for about five seconds and then announced, "I've got a load of little old ladies to take shopping."

As quickly as she appeared, Wendy swept out of my office, leaving Len and me in the blue haze of smoke.

"Doesn't anyone around here knock?" Len grumbled as he pulled out his chrome tool and snuffed the tobacco plug. He briefly looked at my overflowing wastebasket and decided not to dump the ashes there. "I suppose it's my own fault for not locking the door when I walked in."

"Most people don't lock their rooms," I said. "Anyone can walk in and most of the residents welcome the visitors. There wasn't any sign of forced entry to Axel's apartment, so the killer either walked in through the unlocked door or Axel let the killer in."

"It might be time for change," Len replied.

"At this point, it would be like closing the barn doors after the horses are out."

"I'd prefer you think of it as getting smart and take heed of the warning," Len replied as he pulled the lighter out again. He put the lighter back in his pocket and clamped the pipe between his teeth. "Don't worry, I'm not going to light it."

Wendy appeared at my door, her face flushed and slightly out of breath. "Could you give Jenny a hand? I just called the ambulance. We'll need some help getting Lloyd Borczik onto a gurney."

It's hard to explain how a burst of adrenaline affects me, but my pain was on the back burner as the three of us quickly hustled to the stairs and ran to the second floor. "What happened to Gup?" Len asked.

"Gup?" I asked

"Back in high school, Lloyd was the halfback for the football team," Len explained as he caught his breath. "He wasn't very good, and he fumbled at least once in every game. Someone said he was the opposite of Pug Lund, the famous all-American football player for the University of Minnesota, so everyone started calling him Gup. Pug backwards."

Len continued as we walked down the hall. "Gup was a muscular man who'd worked the railroad until a rail coupling mangled his right hand. That all happened before I was born and my early memories of Gup were of him standing behind the counter in his butcher shop wearing a blood-stained apron. Every kid who went into the store would rush to the end of the counter where Gup stocked wieners. Gup called the kids little beggars, but would dole out a coarse-ground wiener to each of us with a smile. I remember the wieners being tiny in his ham-sized left hand. He was probably the only one-handed butcher in Minnesota."

Inside the apartment Jenny was standing beside Gup who was stretched out on his recliner. He looked pasty and was drenched in sweat. At first, I thought he was unconscious, but his eyes popped open when we approached his chair.

"Hey, Len," Gup said, ignoring the rest of us. "I guess I must've had one too many meatballs." Saying those few words left him breathless.

"Gup, I can still see you in the butcher shop making meatballs." For the benefit of the rest of us, Len made a circular motion over his stomach. "Gup made the best meatballs. He'd grab big lumps of hamburger in his good hand and roll them on his bare stomach."

A smile flickered on Gup's face. "That gave them extra flavor."

Jenny gave a furtive glance to Gup's barrel chest and rolled her eyes. "I'd think the board of health would object to that technique."

"Let me tell you, honey, my belly is a lot more sanitary than the meat scraps that go into most sausage."

Gup took a sudden deep breath and arched his back. He writhed in pain and his face turned ashen. Behind me, Len called the dispatcher and asked if the ambulance was near.

"C'mon," Jenny said. "Let's get him on the floor."

The four of us struggled to get Gup out of his recliner and lying flat. Jenny pulled a blood pressure cuff out of her pocket and wrapped it around Gup's arm. His color got a little better when Wendy slipped a pillow under his feet, although he continued to take shallow breaths.

"What do you think?" Gup asked Jenny. "Am I going to be on the same side of the sod as Axel?"

Jenny, who is the most reassuring person I've ever known, was searching for the right words.

Gup closed his eyes and nodded. "I thought it was that bad."

He struggled to catch another breath as another wave of pain grabbed him. Beads of sweat glistened on his forehead and he clutched his chest with his huge left hand. I was struck with the terrible thought that I'd have to plan funerals in two consecutive weeks. Gup relaxed, and I thought he'd breathed his last, but he drew in another breath.

The whine of the ambulance siren was getting close and I hoped they were close enough. Gup was taking rapid shallow breaths, and his eyes didn't open again. Jenny took his blood pressure again, then took a second reading. She looked at Len and bit her bottom lip as I bolted to meet the EMTs at the front door.

Thankfully, Gup had a little color and was breathing more easily when the EMTs wheeled him through the lobby. The hum of the voices in the lobby stopped when the gurney rolled past; the only sounds were the hiss of the oxygen mask over Gup's face and the squeaking of a gurney wheel that needed oil.

Howard Johnson was standing next to me in our silent vigil. When the doors closed behind the EMTs he took a deep breath. "I wish you'd have the ambulance come to the back door. I hate the regular reminders of my own mortality."

Len walked up behind us as activity returned to the lobby. "Howard, I've been talking to the guys at the barber shop and everyone has theory about Axel's murder. What do you know about Axel's gold mine?"

I marveled at the value of Len's experience. I wouldn't have gone to the barber shop for information, but the two hubs of all city gossip were the barber shop and the beauty parlor. There wasn't a secret in Two Harbors that hadn't been passed at one of those venues.

"Some stories never die," Howard said, shaking his head slowly. "Axel was running all over the region buying up ugly landlocked pieces of land at sheriff's auctions for bargain-basement prices. The rumors were raging from the uranium speculation of the '80s to the paper pulp shortages of the '90s. Axel's land always seemed to lack an access easement, which made them useless for anything but helicopter logging. Axel told people that someday someone would find precious minerals, or diamonds, or uranium, and when they did, the state and county would certainly provide an easement so the minerals could be mined. In the meanwhile, he argued with the tax assessors about the valuation of swampy timberland without road access."

"What about the gold?" I asked.

"What about it?" Howard replied. "There are veins of minerals all over northern Minnesota. Hematite and taconite are in the Mesabi Range. Copper and nickel deposits are near the Boundary Waters. I suppose if a guy had enough parcels of land in a checkerboard around valuable mineral land, eventually you'd find yourself sitting on top of a vein of some mineral. My guess is that the mineral deposits you find most often around here are gravel that's salted with a few Lake Superior agates. Last I heard, agates were going for about five bucks a pound."

Howard paused, looking at my shirt. "Peter, if you don't have a spare shirt here, I'll loan you one. In the meanwhile, could you take your vomit-stained shirt away from the dining room?"

I think I was so tired that I didn't even turn red. I nodded numbly. "I've got a Hawaiian shirt in the car that I used for our luau dinner. I'll put it on."

The cold wind seemed almost cathartic as I stood next to the car and stripped off my once-white shirt. A wolf whistle caught my attention. I spun around and saw Miriam walking Tucker behind my car.

"Nice abs, Peter," she said. If you worked out a little you could have a nice six-pack." Tucker bumbled along happily, stopping next to me to shake his head, beating my shins with his flopping ears.

My headache and fatigue prevented a witty retort. I fished the gaudy Hawaiian shirt out of my trunk and shook it twice in an unsuccessful attempt to get rid of the wrinkles.

"I heard you knocked your noggin," Miriam said, guiding Tucker between the cars. She was about five-three and had an ageless look that made me think she could be a couple years older than I was, or she could've been my mother's age. She looked up at the bandage that Jenny had taped over the butterflies on my forehead. While Miriam was light-hearted, and lent an air of fun to the kitchen staff, she could also be matronly and compassionate. She touched the bridge of my nose lightly.

"Honey, you're going to have a raccoon mask for a couple weeks."

"It'll be a nice look for the funeral," I replied.

"Don't get too worked up over Axel's funeral," she said, tugging at Tucker's leash in an attempt to stop him from rolling on spot in the grass that had piqued his interest. He responded by standing upright and shaking his head, which caused his ears to flap. "He wasn't worth the effort that you're putting out."

"That's right, you're not an Axel fan either."

"Axel was like my drug-dealing neighbor in the Nevada trailer court," she replied. "No one cared if he were alive or dead. His passing was just the loss of a boil from the butt of humanity."

"Anything besides the groping incident that makes you say that?"

"Nope, just a couple years of exposure to him," she said. "He wasn't worth the worry that he caused, although he wanted people to think that he was." Tucker was sniffing at a few deer pellets that were strewn on the grass and Miriam pulled him away before he could eat or roll on them. "There is one good thing that's come out of Axel's death."

"What would that be?"

"It's given the residents a fourth discussion topic," she said. Tucker loped over to my tire and peed.

"What are the other three topics?"

"Well, grandchildren are probably first, followed by the food."

"Wait! Let me guess. The weather is topic three."

"Peter, don't you ever listen when you walk through the dining room?"

"Sure. I hear people talking about the food and grandkids. So, what's number three?"

"Bowel movements."

"You're kidding."

"Nope. You go full circle and you worry about the basics, like poop."

"Are you Tucker's new parent?" I asked, seizing an opportunity to move on to another subject.

She shrugged. "I'm not sure yet. He's OK most of the time. Do you have any idea what kind of mix he is? I mean, he's got the short legs and long ears of a basset, but his hair is too long and the color isn't right."

"Axel said he was basset hound and Saint Bernard."

The right corner of her mouth curled just enough to hint at a smile. "You're joking."

"Axel said he was a tribute to the triumph of the little guy over the big guy."

"I've got to tell you, Peter, in all my years of farming I've never seen animals with that much size difference breed. There's a whole lot of anatomy and physics that says that's not possible. I can buy basset and beagle, but not the Saint Bernard."

"Maybe if the dad had a little stool."

"Peter, you are such a city kid."

"Tucker still needs a home, regardless of his lineage," I said, quickly turning the conversation before it went in another direction that might violate some workplace rule.

"I'm not sure that I'm ready for an additional long-term commitment."

"The farm, a husband, and this job are enough for you?"

Miriam's eyes crinkled as she smiled, making me think she might be closer to forty. "If only you knew." She patted me on the arm and walked away with Tucker loping along happily at her side.

My office phone was ringing when I returned. Caller ID said that it was a northern Minnesota cell phone. I picked it up, not anticipating the hornet's nest I was about to step into.

"Peter! This is going to cost you big!" Wendy seethed.

"Settle down and tell me what's going on." It took me a second to remember that she'd taken a vanload of residents on a shopping trip to Miller Hill Mall in Duluth.

"We're in the van, sitting in front of the mall, and I have two missing little old ladies. It's twenty minutes past the time we agreed to meet and they're nowhere in sight."

"Did you contact mall security?"

"Not yet," Wendy replied, a little of the gale-force winds coming out of her sails.

"Go to the security office, tell them who is missing and give them a description. Call me back in ten minutes."

"I hate you," she said as the line went dead.

My impatient ten-minute wait ended. I grabbed the phone on the first ring. "Wendy, did you find them?"

"Security did. They were sitting in a corner booth in the burger place and they lost track of time after their third chocolate martinis."

"They were drinking?"

"Hey, they're drunk. I got the security guys to help me pour them into their seats and they're now happily snoring. I don't know exactly what this is going to cost you, but it'll be big."

"Settle down," I said, before I realized that I was talking to a dial tone.

Chapter 27

The vanload of Duluth shoppers returned just as the dining room was opening for supper. A sea of gray-haired women stepped down from the van, then jostled for position to catch the elevator ahead of the others so they could stash their purchases before returning for supper. I found myself standing next to Howard Johnson, who was standing next to the aviary, watching the hubbub.

"Peter, did you notice who didn't go to Duluth?" he asked as Wendy carefully unloaded a wheelchair using the mechanical lift. She was focused, and I quickly made plans to hide before she started hunting for me.

I looked at the people trooping past and didn't notice anything out of the ordinary. All of the van's sixteen seats had been filled. "I guess I don't understand your question, Howard. There are nearly one hundred residents and only sixteen fit on the van. There are about eighty-five people who didn't go to Duluth. That's not a very exclusive group."

"Look there," he said, nodding toward the dining room entrance.

Hulda Packer was pushing her rolling walker into the dining room, a brilliant green and red scarf draped over her dowager's hump. As usual, it complemented her ivory dress.

"I guess I don't see anything out of sorts," I replied.

"Hulda never misses the shopping bus, Peter. She lives for her clothes, and she didn't even put her name on the standby list for the Duluth van." We stood there in silence for a bit, then he added, "She's been a little too disinterested in Axel's demise."

"Huh?"

"Try to keep up, Peter. She's too aloof. She's snooping around the edges of all the conversations, trying to glean tidbits about the state of the investigation."

I caught the scent of pipe smoke just before Len Rentz startled me by asking, "Who's snooping around the investigation?"

Howard Johnson took Len's sudden appearance in stride and said, "Hulda Packer, the woman with the dowager's hump."

Len assessed Hulda and shook his head. "She looks more like a poisoner than a stabber."

Howard shrugged. "Think what you want, but Hulda is a force with which to be reckoned." He hesitated, and then said to me, "I understand that you contacted my great-niece about the bagpiper on her website."

"I contacted your niece?"

"That's what she said. She was surprised to see that someone had contacted her from here, so she called to ask if I knew who Musicman@WhistlingPines.com would be, and I told her that could only be you, Peter."

"I don't recall contacting a website about bagpipers."

A broad smile crept across Howard's face. "She runs a phone sex operation out of Canada and uses one of her employees, who happens to be a female bagpiper, as the logo on her homepage." He gave me a knowing wink.

The van was completely unloaded and Wendy was guiding the two tipsy passengers past us into the dining room. They were both still staggering a bit as they went past, just in time for Wendy to catch the end of the conversation.

I could feel the color rising in my face as Wendy asked, "Your niece does phone sex?"

"I guess it's quite lucrative," Howard said, with obvious pride. "And she's quite insulated from the...er...customers."

He was reveling in my discomfort. I was at a loss for words. He added, "And none of her customers know that she's actually in her 60s and looks like Roseanne Barr. She tells me that it's all about the voice, and her voice is like pure sensual silk."

"Howard, it seems unlikely that you'd be related to someone that Peter would randomly stumble across in Canada," Wendy said.

"It's not unlikely at all," Howard replied. "Branches of my family have been in northern Minnesota and southern Manitoba for a hundred years. There weren't many people here and the few families had many children who intermarried a lot."

Len chuckled and played dumb. "Phone sex. Really, Peter?"

"Honest to God," I said to Howard. "I was trying to find bagpipers and when I did the Internet search, it directed me to that website. She's playing a bagpipe."

"What's she wearing, Peter?" Len asked with a sparkle in his eye.

"She's wearing a kilt," Wendy said.

"Is she wearing anything else?" Howard asked, obviously aware of the topless piper on the website.

I tried to give him the look but it came off more like I had gas. "Um, bagpipes, I guess."

Howard winked at me and walked off to dinner.

Wendy broke out in a big grin, "She found a mechanic to work on her van and they have parts coming from Winnipeg. I can hardly wait until she gets here!" She hustled off toward the dining room, so smug about the Canadian piper that she forgot about how angry she was with me.

Chapter 28

Friday

Between the headache and anxiety over the funeral plans I'd hardly slept when I awoke Friday morning. In the last moments of sleep I had been dreaming that as Axel's hearse pulled in front of the church, dark clouds started to gather and a lightning bolt hit the steeple. Smoke was seeping from the edges of the casket, and I awoke drenched in sweat to the smell of burning sulphur. After quickly checking the house for fire, I decided I'd smelled brimstone arising from Axel's eternal damnation.

I reluctantly looked into the mirror and was dismayed at the dark rings around my eyes. Blood had soaked through the gauze on my forehead, which was painful to pull free. The wound could only be described as a gash. It started to ooze around the butterfly bandages Jenny had applied and as soon as the gauze was off I questioned the wisdom of not visiting the emergency room. A couple of stitches would've stopped the bleeding. I struggled to replace the bandage and ended up with a wad of gauze stuck under a cross of adhesive tape, a pretty pathetic effort for a guy who had patched up many nasty wounds with practiced precision. This mess looked like it had been assembled by a third grader. In my own defense I rationalized that I'd never tried to bandage myself while looking in a mirror.

I cut myself shaving, slipped in the shower and bruised my butt in the fall. The filter in my Mr. Coffee folded over, leaving my cup filled with coffee grounds. Karma said that this was going to be one hell of a day. I was at work by daylight, and the looks from the residents confirmed that I probably looked worse than I felt. Jenny showed up in my office with fresh gauze and tape while I was confirming the bus arrangements for the funeral with Enos, who was not pleased at being rousted from bed, even though he was supposed to be at the door in less than an hour.

"Peter, you should've left the old gauze on for another day," Jenny said as she closed the office door before gently pulling the gauze free, causing another round of pain.

"The blood had seeped through the gauze. I thought it looked tacky."

"So, a wad of gauze taped on with ten-inch strips of tape that run from your ear up into your hairline looks better?" she asked as she stepped back to inspect her repairs.

"The blood-soaked toilet paper on your jaw is very attractive, too." She pulled that free in pieces that appeared to be the size of a dime. She dabbed at the razor cut with gauze and then put a extra-large band-aid on that wound too. Again, she inspected her handiwork and lifted my chin to better inspect my blackened eyes.

"That tree really did a number on you."

"Mmm. You were probably right. I should've gone to the ER for some stitches."

"Probably should've had a CT scan to make sure you don't have a concussion, too," she replied. "Are you all set for the funeral?" she asked as she released my chin.

"I have no idea. I've been planning, but Wendy seems to be running her own agenda. The church changed, the revised obituary was in the newspaper, and the Ladies Aide supposedly called all the local seniors' residences to tell them about the change to Duluth. Wendy's cousin, Enos, is coming to pick up the residents and deliver them to the Duluth church. We may or may not have a hooker coming to play bagpipes. She may not know about the change of church, and I'm not sure that immigration and customs will allow her into the country. We still don't know who killed Axel, but the list of people with motives only gets longer. Axel's children, illegitimate and otherwise, hated him and are unhappy with me personally." I paused and tallied up the situation. "Yes, that pretty well covers it."

"Is there anything positive going on?"

I thought for another second. "Nope. Not one positive thing comes to mind. That is, unless you consider the possibility of a job change because I'm going to be fired."

"It'll be fine," she said, pulling me up from my office chair. "It's time for the funeral, come what may."

I took a step toward the door when it flew open, slamming into my face and sending me reeling. I stumbled back into the chair and sat hard, rolling back into the computer desk where I knocked the keyboard and mouse to the floor with my elbow. At first, I was too shocked to register pain, but that blissful state quickly passed into one of searing pain.

"Oh, sorry," Wendy said as she stepped into the office. "Enos's bus is here."

I was trying to see straight when a wave of nausea swept over me. Jenny jumped to my aid and quickly advised me to take some deep breaths. She grabbed gauze from the first aid kit and she held it under my nose.

"Uh oh," Wendy said, watching the emergency first aid. "Have you got another shirt, Peter?"

I looked down as Jenny tried to staunch the blood flowing from my nose onto the front of my freshly pressed, blue button-down shirt.

"I can't go to the funeral in a bloody shirt, and I don't have enough time to go home for a fresh one."

"Hang on," Wendy said as she swept out of the office. While she was gone, Jenny pressed the gauze against my nose and told me to hold it there. While I was holding the gauze she made a pair of gauze plugs that she pressed into my nostrils.

In less than a minute, Wendy was back with a Hawaiian shirt even gaudier than the one I'd worn the previous day. "Here, Peter," she said, holding the shirt out to me. "I had my luau shirt behind the door in my office. You can wear it to the funeral."

I stared at the wild pattern of bright red and yellow flowers on dark green leaves. Wendy was "full-figured" so there was no question that the shirt was large enough, but it was also cut to accommodate her ample bosom. Jenny and Wendy had me in the shirt before I could protest, and we were on our way to the front door to meet the bus.

We met Margaret "Maggie" Alden in the hallway, pushing her walker toward her room. She stopped us and grabbed me by the sleeve of the Hawaiian shirt. She suffered from a degenerative eye condition that was slowly stealing her eyesight. She pulled me close and examined my bruised, bloody face.

"You're so ugly you make my eyes hurt," she said, releasing me before continuing down the hall.

I looked at Wendy who wore a broad smile. "She's right."

By the time we reached the lobby the bus was idling under the portico and the residents were gathering in the lobby. Hulda Packer was speaking loudly to a group of women, all dressed in their new funeral outfits. Nearly half of them had price tags flagging from the cuffs.

I touched Busty McAllen's shoulder. A look of horror crossed her face when she saw the Hawaiian shirt. I was a little relieved that the shirt was more noticeable than my face.

"The price tag is still on the cuff of your dress," I said. "Can I get a scissors and cut if off for you?"

She looked absently at the tag, then turned to me with a scowl. "Peter, I'm not keeping this dress. I have to leave the tag on or the store won't let me return it after the funeral." Several of the other women were nodding. I had enough on my platter without dealing with the moral incorrectness of returning worn clothing, so I nodded and went on my way.

Wendy was directing people from the dining room onto the bus, while Jenny was making sure that everyone had taken their morning medications before departure. Everything seemed to be rolling along like a well-oiled machine without my help, which made me relieved and at the same time, after the chaos of the last few days, a little under-appreciated. I faded into the background and watched the whole scene. To my enormous surprise, Gup Borczik came out of the elevator pulling a green oxygen bottle. I'd never seen Gup in anything but a plaid shirt with a white T-shirt showing at the neck, but today he was wearing a white shirt and blue necktie that featured a hand-painted rainbow trout. I glanced at his injured hand and wondered how he'd managed to knot the tie.

"Lloyd, I thought you'd still be in the hospital," I said, falling into step alongside Gup as he made his way to the bus.

"Doctor said I was probably just having gas pains and wanted me to hang around a couple more days, but I wanted to see Axel get planted."

My surprise must have shown because Gup smiled. "I really don't give a shit about the funeral. I just want to make sure that it's really Axel in the coffin, and that it gets buried. It's hard to believe that some of us outlived that son of a bitch."

"Don't tell me that Axel wronged you too."

"Gup held up his right hand with the three twisted fingers. "Axel had nothing to do with this," he said, "but he called me "Claw" one day. I surprised him by grabbing his collar with my good hand and throwing him into the street. He tried to blackball me, spreading rumors that I was selling tainted meat and that I had hepatitis, but I had my regulars, who hated Axel as much as I did, and my business got better, if anything."

"Who else hated Axel?" I asked.

Gup shook his head. "It's easier to count the ones who liked him. That count would be none."

I'm not sure if it was the pain or the fatigue that led me to ask, "Did you hate Axel enough to kill him?"

Gup's face was blank as he looked off toward the throng at the door. The oxygen whispered a hiss from the green tube under his nose and a large vein throbbed in his neck as I waited for a response. He paused so long that I was beginning to think he either wasn't going to answer, or he was going to unleash the giant left fist that he was clenching. He finally took a deep breath, exhaled slowly and relaxed his fist.

"Peter, if I'd killed Axel, I would've strangled him," he said, focusing on a point somewhere over my head. "I think I would have liked to see his eyes bug out as he slowly recognized he was going to die for all the manure that he'd spread on people's lives."

Gup's eyes met mine and I could see calmness there. "I thought I was going to meet my maker yesterday, Peter, and I think that Axel's going to get his payback elsewhere. I saw my wife, my parents, old friends, and lots of my customers waiting for me with smiles on their faces as I faded out. I think that isn't the group that met Axel as he passed from this life. I suspect Axel smelled burning brimstone and was met by a man who had other plans for Axel's eternity." Gup smiled and gently squeezed my right hand with his massive left one before stepping into the line for the bus as I remembered my morning dream.

Kathy, the director, flew through the lobby looking harried and issuing orders to anyone who would listen. "Oh, Peter," she said, stopping in front of me and taking in the sorry state of my appearance from black eyes to bandages and Hawaiian shirt. "You're going to the funeral like that?"

Before I could answer there was a crashing of dishes from the dining room and Kathy ran to investigate.

Miriam swept out of the dining room with Tucker straining at his leash. She smiled as she passed and said, "Nice nose plugs." I'd never seen Miriam in anything but a white uniform and stained white apron. Her muted mauve blouse and black slacks made her look like a different person.

Tucker seemed focused on making it to the nearest patch of grass, but suddenly stopped and started baying at the crowd. A group of men had just exited the elevator and

Tucker's ire seemed to be directed at them. Miriam tugged the leash and dragged him out the door before I could determine which person irritated Tucker.

Howard Johnson was leading a group of three women when I cornered him before he could get out the door. A few residents still had driver's licenses and Howard was the most generous, often giving others rides to buy groceries or to doctor's appointments. Howard shooed his female passengers toward his Buick LeSabre and returned to meet me. He was dressed in a black suit. The pressed creases in his pants were sharp enough to cut bread and his black shoes were so shiny that they looked baby blue as they reflected the cloudless sky. He wore a tasteful maroon tie with a matching silk kerchief peeking out of his breast pocket.

"Good morning, Peter," he said, carefully assessing my bruised face and the Hawaiian shirt. "You've made an interesting choice of dress for the funeral. I hadn't been informed of the Hawaiian theme."

I wasn't in the mood for levity or small talk. "Did you know that Florie had all kinds of dirt on Axel?" I asked.

Howard's expression quickly shifted from mirth to darkness. "I've told you, Peter, I don't participate in rumor mongering."

"Someone killed Axel because of something he'd done. That's a fact, not a rumor."

Howard looked at the women shuffling to his car, then back at me. "The things that Florie knows about have been simmering for years, maybe even decades. I've been thinking and I had to ask myself why someone would suddenly act on those things after all these years." He looked me in the eye and added, "I heard Axel was stabbed. Sticking a knife into someone is a vicious act of passion. When I was in the war, we all sharpened our bayonets in preparation for that big hand-to-hand fight, but in reality, sticking a knife into another person is not easy. Many soldiers can't do it when their lives are at stake."

"Someone did it this time."

"Someone snapped," Howard said. "Axel pushed someone a step too far and they reacted. This wasn't somebody's historical vendetta that could have been settled years ago."

"Peter!" Wendy called. "Get on the bus. We're loaded and ready to roll."

Howard hurried to catch up with the ladies waiting in his Buick and I climbed onto the bus. I fell into an empty seat that Wendy had saved in the second row of the bus and stared at the now almost empty parking lot. Axel's baby blue Lincoln Town Car with the dented fenders was the only car left in the residents' lot. A shiny bit of metal on a rear fender stood as evidence of his most recent episode of driving by Braille. The employee lot was also nearly empty. I wondered who, if anyone, was still in the building.

We were well on our way to Duluth before I realized that there were men I didn't recognize, dressed in blue blazers and captains' hats, roaming the aisles talking to the passengers. An octogenarian "captain" stopped at the row in front of me and complimented Hulda Packer on her dress. It took awhile, with the blow to my head and double vision, to realize that The Seasick Sailors were on the bus with us, and they were actively chatting up my senior citizens. The warning about the randy sailors rattled around my head like a death knell. I was too tired, too sore, and literally too bleary-eyed to take action. Hulda seemed to be reveling in the attention.

Somewhere in the back of the bus a concertina started to play, and as we passed the Duluth city limits the bus was rocking as everyone sang "The Beer Barrel Polka." The funeral had just morphed into a circus.

Chapter 29

The half-hour-long bus ride gave me time to think about Howard's words. "Someone snapped." Someone with a stiletto at hand stabbed Axel in a fit of anger or passion. I was convinced it wasn't any of the women. Len had pointed out that women tend to choose poison as their murder weapon and Howard had said how difficult it was for even a trained soldier to stab someone. I was one of only three men on the staff, and I couldn't see Jingle or Russell killing anyone. That left the dozen or so male residents and maybe an unexpected guest.

Jenny slid into the seat next to me and patted my knee. "How's the headache?"

"Loud noises make it pound." The busload of revelers was one loud noise.

I looked at the faces around me. Everyone was animated and talkative. A few male residents were on the bus, but most had either driven themselves or ridden with someone. I ran through the list in my head and none of them struck me as enough of a hothead to kill Axel. What would set one of them off?

"Have you ever seen one of the residents get really angry?" I asked.

"A few of them have popped their cork once or twice," Jenny replied. "Why, are you still playing detective?"

"Something Howard Johnson said is resonating in my mind. He said that it's very hard to stab someone with a knife. It would have to be in a fit of extreme anger."

"So, who made Howard a forensic psychologist?"

"He said he'd learned in the service that it is very difficult to stab someone."

Jenny considered that for a moment. "I've never heard him talk about his experiences in the war. As you know, the vets who saw the worst of the fighting don't talk about it."

"The Marines I was with didn't see any hand-to-hand combat in Iraq. By the time I was there, we were mostly dealing with a faceless enemy who remotely detonated roadside bombs."

Astrid Carlson leaned over the seat and asked, "Peter, where did you find the people to play the bagpipes?"

I was struck by a sudden panic attack that rivaled anything I'd felt in Iraq. I stammered, not knowing whether to admit that I didn't have pipers, or whether I should raise the distant chance that the Canadian phone sex operator might make it across the border. The website photo flashed in front of me. I gave Jenny a guilty glance, hoping that she wasn't able to read my mind. At that thought, I felt the crimson start creeping up my neck and my ears started to burn.

"Wendy took care of the arrangements," I blurted out quickly. "She said that the piper is from Winnipeg. Last I heard, the piper was having car problems and she was waiting for car parts."

"Oh, that would be sad," Astrid replied. "We've all got our hopes up."

I opened my mouth, but nothing came out. Finally, the words expressing the reality came to me. "It really doesn't matter anymore, does it?"

Chapter 30

The church's parking lot was about half full when we arrived an hour before the funeral. The official plan was that there would be a one-hour family visitation prior to the funeral service. The people filed off the bus to sign the visitor's book and got in line to express their condolences to the family. Jenny and I were the last two people off the bus.

I was surprised to see my neighbor, Dolores, standing near the front of the line. She wore a black dress that I surmised had been to many funerals and a black pillbox hat that had been new during the Kennedy presidency. Her handbag, big enough to be carry-on luggage, looked like it was made from flowered carpeting. She greeted Axel's daughter and two sons politely, then paused for a second near the open casket with her head bowed.

"Oh dear, the mortician got carried away with the makeup again," she said to no one in particular. She turned to Cassie McGahey, who was standing at the foot of the casket, and said, "I think they used a trowel to put the makeup on. The lipstick isn't the right color for his complexion."

Cassie moved up closer to Dolores and viewed Axel. "Such a pity that he died so young."

Dolores looked at Cassie with surprise. "He wasn't young. They colored his hair and filled his wrinkles with pancake makeup."

Hulda Packer pushed between the two women and steadied herself on the edge of the casket. She leaned over the edge and studied Axel. "Hmph. You can't even tell that his nose is plastic."

Cassie frowned. "I didn't know he had a plastic nose."

"Oh yes," Hulda said. "His nose was almost blown off in the war and they had to replace it with plastic."

"I think you have him confused with Ernie Pascal," Dolores said.

Hulda looked in the casket again and leaned back. "Well then, I guess that's why it looks so real."

"Hello, Dolores," I said as she turned from the casket. "I didn't expect you to attend the funeral. You didn't like him very much. Dolores grabbed the sleeve of the Hawaiian shirt, pulling me close for examination through her Coke-bottle-bottom eyeglasses.

"Is that you, Peter?"

"Yes, Dolores, it's me."

"Well, I didn't like Axel, but that has nothing to do with going to a funeral. Weddings and funerals are the only time I get to see my friends. What happened to your face, and why are you wearing that hideous shirt?" Dolores had never been one to filter her thoughts.

"I ran into a tree branch yesterday and knocked myself out. The shirt is another story."

"Why are you wearing a woman's blouse?" She asked, examining the darts in the front. "Are you having a sex change?"

"No, I had a nosebleed on my other shirt and one of the women was nice enough to loan me this shirt."

Dolores looked around the room, examining people as carefully as she could. "I don't see anyone without a blouse."

"It was her spare one. I didn't take the blouse she was wearing."

"Well, if she had spare blouses, why did you take that hideous one? Didn't she have something tasteful?"

I heard snickering behind me and found Wendy at my shoulder, doing all she could to suppress full guffaws.

"Did you give Peter this hideous blouse?" Dolores asked Wendy.

Wendy sidled up to Dolores and put her arm around Dolores's hunched shoulders. "Isn't it just terrible that Peter would wear something like that to a funeral?" Wendy asked.

"Tasteless," Dolores replied. "If he wasn't such a nice neighbor, I might've suggested that the funeral director ask him to leave the church."

"Wendy, don't you have to start the background music?" I asked, hoping to move on.

"Good idea, Peter," she replied. "I spoke with Axel's daughter," she pointed to Christine and her mountain of blonde hair. She wore skin-tight black leather pants and black cowboy boots with rhinestone studs. It was obviously the perfect grieving outfit in Texas. "She said 'Penny Lane' would be just fine. As a matter of fact, she said I could play any damn thing I wanted as long as it was short and we could get out of this church before the rafters caved in because Axel was here."

Axel's sons were wearing traditional black suits. There was no sign of spouses or children. Apparently, Dad's funeral wasn't enough of an event to disrupt the entire family for a day. Gary looked at me and shrugged. I took that to mean that he'd never heard back from whomever he'd tried to contact for a military honor guard.

"Penny Lane?" Dolores asked. "Is that something from Gilbert and Sullivan? I do enjoy their music."

"Actually, it's something from the Beatles," Wendy replied. "They are wonderfully talented musicians and it's a very catchy tune about a barber shop. It'll probably remind you of Gilbert and Sullivan."

"Oh, how quaint," Dolores said, shifting her purse to keep in firmly mounted on her shoulder. "Will that be after or before the bagpipes?"

"Oh, it'll be before," Wendy said, giving me a wink. "I'm saving the bagpipes for the recessional."

I felt a sudden queasiness and decided to step outside for a breath of fresh air. That wasn't a terribly good idea because the front of the church was crowded with people waiting in line to view the open casket. I found Miriam and Tucker on the fringe of the group.

"I didn't expect Tucker to be at the funeral," I said as I maneuvered myself away from the blue cloud coming from the dozen or so smokers who were getting their nicotine fix before entering the church, and watched the slow parade of tourists driving down London Road, the route that ran along Lake Superior. A few cars pulled into the church and cruised the nearly full parking lot for one of the few remaining open slots.

Miriam shrugged. "It seemed like he was as much a part of Axel's family as any of the kids who never visited him."

"Are you planning to take him inside for the service?" As I asked, Tucker decided that was the proper moment to flop on his side and lick himself.

Miriam watched the licking display and shrugged. "I think I'll play that by ear."

"You might want to find him a tire before you walk down the aisle. He seems to find tires irresistible, and you wouldn't want him sizing up the end of a pew for a squirt."

"Yeah, squirting the pews would be bad. Drinking the holy water might be worse."

"Lutherans don't use holy water," I said.

"Good. There probably aren't any prayer candles for him to eat, either. We might be safe"

Dozens of other potential doggie misdeeds raced through my brain. I decided to play dumb. "Where is Tucker going after the funeral?" I asked as horns sounded on the roadway. A large tour bus, towing a trailer, was blocking the northbound traffic lane, waiting for an opening in the continuous southbound flow. I briefly wondered which church group or seniors' residence felt the need to bring a trailer behind their load of funeral attendees.

"No one seems to want him," Miriam said, scratching Tucker behind a flopping ear. "I guess he'll have to come to the farm."

The crowd parted behind Miriam as Axel's daughter pressed her way through, shaking a cigarette from a pack. She held a Bic lighter to the end and inhaled deeply, before spying me.

"Are you the caterer or something?" she asked as she blew smoke into my face. Tucker was at her feet, sniffing her shoes and being his usual inquisitive doggy self.

"I'm Peter, from Whistling Pines. We met last week to talk about the funeral arrangements."

She looked at my bandaged forehead, black eyes, flowered shirt, and plugged nose, then drew deeply on the cigarette. "Oh, I remember you. Did some woman clock you for staring at her boobs?"

I focused my entire energy on keeping eye contact, willing myself not to stare down at the great white expanse of cleavage being pressed upward by unknown engineering forces.

She took a third drag on the cigarette as the organ music started inside the church. After blowing a stream of blue smoke skyward she dropped her cigarette and ground it out under the toe of her cowboy boot. "I guess it's finally time to get this over with," she said as she turned on her heel and left.

I followed the crowd toward the front doors. As I neared the doors, I heard the rattling sound of a wheezing car engine and looked back to see an aged minivan trailing blue smoke pulling in behind the tour bus.

"Oh, man," I said to no one. "I wonder if that's the van from Winnipeg?" I asked as the tour bus circled the church driveway searching for a bus-sized parking spot.

By the time I got into the sanctuary every seat was taken, so I slid to the back corner near a stored baptismal font. Len Rentz was already there wearing a black suit and fiddling with his pipe. The casket was closed. The minister mounted the step to the pulpit and cleared his throat. The three members of Axel's family sat in the front row. I was surprised to see Florie sitting about four feet away from them in the same pew.

"Len," I whispered. "Why is Florie in the front row?"

"The family met with Axel's lawyer yesterday. It seems that Florie is Axel's illegitimate child from the time he was in Georgia."

"Is that why she came to Minnesota?"

"I guess she was quite a pistol as a teenager, and her mom sent her to be with Axel, knowing he wouldn't take any grief from her."

"I bet it was a shock for the other three children."

"They didn't welcome her with open arms," Len whispered. "She has a chance to get a full quarter of Axel's estate, and the rest thought it would be a three-way split. Of course, that's assuming they meet the success clause in the will."

"What's the success clause?"

"Each of the children gets money to invest. If they double the seed money they can come back to the trustee and get increasing disbursements for investment."

"And if they're not successful, what happens?"

"It sounds like there is a time limit. If they don't meet the targets, the trustee has the discretion to redirect shares to the more successful siblings."

"Oh, I bet that will draw the children closer together."

"Based on what you know about Axel, does any of that surprise you?"

"Since he couldn't take it with him, Axel decided to keep his grasp on it, even after he died."

Len put a finger to his lips and pointed to the minister.

The minister arranged his notes and took a deep breath. "We're here to remember a man who had a great impact on this community. I never knew Axel, since he wasn't a church-going man, but it's quite apparent that he touched many lives by looking over the sea of faces that fill this sanctuary."

I was quite impressed that the minister was able to deliver two sentences that did not praise Axel, nor piss off anyone. My senior citizens were squirming in their seats like children, and I saw several of them adjusting hearing aids. For the most part, everyone was civil.

"At the request of the family, I'll be brief. Axel was born in Finland to Swedish parents. He served with honor in the British Intelligence Service during World War Two. He rejoined the British Army during the Korean War, and was awarded the Distinguished Service Order for bravery during a mission behind Chinese lines at the Chosin Reservoir. After the war he emigrated to his adopted country, the United States."

With that news, a murmur spread through the crowd. My seniors, many being nearly deaf, murmured very loudly. At one point a woman turned to Millie Peterson and told her to shut up. The minister waited patiently for the crowd to settle.

"Axel was as astute at business as he was at gathering military intelligence, and he amassed quite a fortune in his adopted country. I understand that he had the rare ability to rub anyone the wrong way." At that point, people actually laughed. "I also understand he never went out of his way to make friends. He spent many hours cruising the roads of northern Minnesota in his vintage Lincoln in search of his next deal. It sounds like he had a lonely existence."

After a brief prayer, Wendy sang "Penny Lane" to the amazement of the crowd, who were all trying to hear the words, and then understand why that song had been chosen. The minister had a few closing words and asked everyone to join the family in the cemetery next to the church for the interment, which would be followed by a luncheon in the church basement catered by the Two Harbors Lutheran Church Ladies Aide Society. As he finished his remarks, I heard the low drone of bagpipes, and looked at

Wendy, who was sitting at the organ, poised to play Loch Lomond. Her expression told me that she was as surprised as I was by the now gathering "groan" of pipes. The drone quickly changed into a melody and "Amazing Grace" echoed throughout the church.

Motion at the back of the church caught my eye. A military honor guard marched down the aisle, followed by a sergeant major, as the bagpipes continued. They marched to a slow cadence tapped out by unseen drummers outside the church. The soldiers' uniforms were British, like those I'd seen in southern Iraq, and the honor guard advanced with a strutting march to a cadence called by a sergeant major. They flanked Axel's coffin. The parishioners rose as the honor guard lifted the coffin to their shoulders and carried it down the aisle in a halting half-step march, followed by Axel's children.

I ducked out a side door and saw eight pipers, in kilts and berets, lining the steps. The military pallbearers eased down the steps. After they passed, the pipers fell in behind them, playing a new dirge as Jenny edged next to me and held my hand.

"Do you recognize that song?" Jenny asked as we fell in behind the family and marched toward the cemetery.

"Oft in the Stilly Night," I said. "It was played at the Queen Mother's funeral."

The awestruck congregation followed. Once regrouped at the gravesite, the minister said a few words, then seven soldiers fired a twenty-one-gun salute. A flock of startled geese erupted from a small pond behind the cemetery at the sound of the guns. Tears welled in my eyes as I thought back to Iraq when I'd watched marines load flag-draped coffins onto military transport planes.

Wendy and Jenny were beside me watching the geese fly off. Jenny said, "You sure kept this all a secret," as the honor guard folded a Union Jack and the sergeant major handed it to Axel's daughter as a bugler played taps.

I brushed the tears aside and admitted, "I'd like to take credit, but I had no idea."

As the crowd broke up, people came past and slapped me on the back. Kathy, the director of Whistling Pines, was wiping tears from her eyes when she stopped at my side. "You did a wonderful job, Peter. I've never been so moved by a funeral." She left again before I could set her straight.

As people approached the cemetery gate, a new drone started and a light jig that I recognized as "Brennan's Reel" started playing near the side door of the church. It took me a few moments to get through the crowd, but I got a glimpse of blonde hair sticking out of a tam-o-shanter. I felt a sickening dread that the phone sex operator was standing there, half naked, playing her heart out like we were having an Irish wake. I pushed through the crowd, and was relieved to see that she was wearing a neatly starched white shirt over her plaid kilt.

"Tucker! Tucker!" I could hear Miriam yelling after the dog who was baying as if he was on a rabbit's scent. She kept calling the dog and got more frantic. "Tucker, get back here!" The dog was baying somewhere across the expansive parking lot.

Jenny and I pushed through the crowd moving toward the church luncheon and rushed toward the far side of parking lot. I came around a full-sized van just in time to see Tucker furiously gnawing on Toivo Saari's ankle. Mirian tried to grab the leash that was flopping around like a wounded snake. I was trying to understand Toivo's Finnish rant when I saw him tug at something behind his head. He pulled a small stiletto and was about to throw it at Tucker when all hell broke loose.

Dolores had hobbled up the sidewalk from the cemetery service. When she saw the knife she wrestled a long-barreled handgun from her carpetbag purse. The gun barrel swung wildly as she tried to aim the barrel in Toivo's direction while keeping her balance. I pushed Jenny behind a car and told her to stay down.

A great white cloud of smoke belched from the antique black powder pistol as the gunshot boomed, followed by the whine of a ricocheting bullet. People started screaming and ducking as Dolores struggled to cock the hammer a second time with her twisted arthritic hands. The scene played out in slow motion as she brought the gun up again, taking aim at Toivo. I found myself once again running toward the sound of the gunfire.

The knife clattered to the ground as Toivo staggered toward his car. Tucker, still attacking, his ears flopping, snarled and tried for a new grip on Toivo's skinny ankle. Dolores waved the gun around in Toivo's general direction, trying to line up her next shot. Through the screaming, and her deafness, my shouts of warning were useless.

The gun roared a second time, belching sparks and smoke, and the hood ornament on Shorty Anderson's old Thunderbird, parked next to Toivo's car, exploded into a thousand tiny pieces that rattled against the windows of Toivo's car. I seemed to be moving in slow motion, dodging between cars like a broken field runner, trying to get to Dolores before she took a third shot. Miriam finally grabbed the leash and pulled Tucker away from the field of fire. I was only one car away, but Dolores had the gun cocked again, and was starting to take aim at Toivo, who was now trying to shield his '57 Chevy from the gunfire with his body while he yelled Finnish invectives at Dolores, spitting snuff all over the hood of the car.

A hand appeared out of the swirling cloud of black powder smoke and lifted the gun gently, but firmly, from Dolores's shaking hand. The sergeant major pointed the gun skyward and gently set the hammer down as Len Rentz reached the scene. Len picked up the stiletto. Miriam held Tucker, who was amazingly unfazed by the gunfire and other commotion, and whispered soothing things to him.

Len nodded to the British sergeant major. "Thanks." The name tag on the soldier's tunic said "Williamson."

The soldier flipped the pistol expertly and handed it butt first to Len. The gun appeared to be one of the antiques from Dolores' collection, and although I didn't have time to do much analysis, my guess was that it was some sort of an old percussion cap Colt revolver from the Civil War era that probably weighed close to three pounds. "You may want to take care of this antique for the lady."

"With pleasure, sergeant major," Len replied. "That was a very brave move."

The soldier smiled. "I was just lending a hand to this lovely woman. I wouldn't want to see that historic firearm damaged."

I finally arrived at the scene and stood amid the smoky haze, trying to catch my breath. I was having problems processing everything. The first thing that came to mind was to ask Sergeant Major Williamson, "Where did you come from?"

His composure was calming and he stood "at ease." "I'm with the honor guard. I heard the commotion and decided it was best to offer my assistance." His words were carefully chosen and delivered with a charming British accent.

"Yes, thank you. But why are you at the funeral?" I asked.

He smiled. "We were training with your Minnesota National Guard at Camp Ripley when we were ordered by the consulate to provide an honor guard for a British hero."

"Do you bring bagpipes for military training?" I asked.

Williamson smiled. "You Yanks seem to enjoy the pipes, so we bring them along for our marches."

Toivo was sprawled on the hood of his Chevy, still muttering in Finnish and bleeding from hood ornament shrapnel. The whole side of his car was peppered with hood ornament fragments. I helped him slide to the ground, then steadied him while he gasped for air.

"She...almost...killed...me," he said as he squirmed and adjusted his pants.

Dolores seemed more indignant than upset. "You tried to throw your puku at the poor woman," she retorted, pointing at Miriam, who was trying to calm Tucker.

"I was trying to hit Axel's damned dog," Snuffy muttered. "He was trying to bite me again."

"Again?" I asked.

Toivo shook his head. He was truly a man of few words.

"When did the dog bite you?" Len asked.

"After Axel dented my car," Toivo replied, spitting tobacco juice onto the pavement.

"What happened after he dented your car?' Len asked.

"I told him to fix it."

"And that didn't go well?" I asked.

"Not so much."

"So you stabbed him?" Len asked.

"Not right away."

Len was patient and waited for Toivo to explain further, but when no futher comments were forthcoming, he asked, "What happened before you stabbed him?"

"Axel walked away."

"And," Len tried to lead him.

Toivo shrugged. "I don't know. I guess I followed him."

"You followed him back to his apartment?" I asked.

"Yup."

"Then what happened?" Len asked, his patience starting to wear thin.

"He got huffy. Told me to leave."

"That's it?" I asked. "Did he say something about your car being old?"

"I don't like people making fun of my car."

"When did the picture get broken?" Len asked.

"Axel started swearing at me in Finnish and I called him a Nazi, 'cause I heard he was a collaborator during the war," Toivo said, his anger starting to take over. "I took his stupid picture off the wall and threw it on the ground. I told him he was no hero."

"What did Axel do when you broke the picture?" I asked.

"He grabbed my collar and told me I didn't know anything. He went to get something out of his desk and I figured he was going for a gun, so I spun him around and stuck him. Then the damned dog bit me."

Len shook his head. "The whole thing started over Axel backing into your car and escalated into Axel trying to kill you?"

"That's it," Toivo replied.

"Axel didn't have a gun in the drawer. I think he was going to show you his medal," Len said.

"The hell, you say," Toivo replied.

Len nodded. "It was a British decoration for heroism."

As Len led Toivo away, I took Dolores by the arm and escorted her across the parking lot toward Jenny. "Dolores, where did you get that pistol?" I asked. "I thought we'd locked all your guns in the cabinet."

Dolores seemed perplexed by the question. "Peter, I always carry that old pistol for self protection. It was in my purse, not the cabinet."

Jenny joined us for the end of the conversation. "Dolores, do you have any other pistols that weren't in the cabinet?" she asked.

"Not any pistols," Dolores replied.

Jenny missed the significance of that comment because Len was calling her name. He motioned for us to join him, so I released Dolores who made a hobbling beeline for the church luncheon.

Chapter 31

Jenny bandaged Toivo's ankle and scratches while he sat in Len's police car.

"Are you arresting Toivo for Axel's murder?" I asked.

"I have to," he replied, "but I doubt the county attorney will file charges. I imagine we'll have to get a public defender for Toivo, and any lawyer worth his weight will argue that Toivo was probably acting in self defense. On top of that, I think he's missing a couple marbles."

"Diminished mental capacity," I said.

Len smiled. "I suppose that would be a polite way of expressing Toivo's mental state."

As Jenny and I walked to the church to see if there was anything left of the lunch, Wendy flew out of the door followed by the blonde Winnipeg piper.

"Peter and Jenny, you have to meet Laura Good." Laura was still in her kilt and tam-o-shanter.

Jenny gave a polite, albeit pained, smile and shook her hand, but she clearly recognized Laura from the website and wasn't entirely pleased to meet her. I shook her hand and noticed her dimples when she smiled at me.

"I'm pleased to meet you, Peter, after all the e-mails we exchanged."

Without peeking at Jenny, I could feel icicles prickling my skin.

"Thank you for coming. I'm really pleased that you could make it for the funeral," I said, wondering how many e-mails Wendy had sent under my name. "Has Wendy made arrangements to pay you for your time?"

"She's already paid my mileage, and she's going to the Mall of America with me for the weekend. We'll have a great time, eh?"

I looked at Wendy, not sure how she got included in the trip to Bloomington. "But, Laura, I thought you had an interest in a Minneapolis convention?" I asked.

"Wendy said we could stay with her aunt in Bloomington and we'll have lots of fun at the mall. She said that they've even got an IKEA there. I can make a killing reselling a van full of IKEA stuff in Canada!" Laura leaned close and pecked me on the cheek. "This has been fun. You guys really know how to throw a funeral!"

Laura and Wendy were off to the parking lot, chatting like schoolgirls.

The bouquet of burning pipe tobacco preceded Len's arrival.

"Thanks for the help with the investigation, Peter. I wouldn't think an argument over a dented bumper would escalate into a murder, but I guess I hadn't considered how adept Axel was at pushing people's hot buttons."

"Well, I didn't realize how psychotic Toivo was about his car," I said.

"The Brits showing up was sure a surprise," Len said. "And I'm amazed that the Canadian girl showed up, and in that interesting outfit. I still wonder what they wear under the kilt."

"Don't you really want to know too?" I asked Jenny with a grin.

"Not at all. Not one bit," Jenny said, shaking her head emphatically.

There was a whistle from the parking lot and Laura and Wendy were waving. When I waved back, Laura spun around and flipped up her kilt.

"Hmm, I didn't know you could get tan lines in Winnipeg this time of year,'" Len observed.

This book is a work of fiction. Any resemblance to actual events is coincidental and unintended. People and places are fictional or used fictionally. Hugo's Bar is real, and if you get the chance to stop off for a beer or to catch some live music, please say "hi" to Tony and Sheila, the owners. Wendy resembles my wife's delightful cousin, Wendy, who sings like an angel. Miriam Milam is a real person who happens to be a human dynamo and the owner of "Off The Farm Products", (I hope the endorsement makes up for describing the Miriam character as sturdy).

Acknowledgements

Every book finds its genesis in a string of experiences, suggestions, and encouragement. I have to credit Brian Johnson, formerly of Two Harbors, for his persistent nudging, for giving me the catalyst that got the creative juices flowing, and for providing a sprinkling of Two Harbors history.

After pecking away at the story for more than a year I wasn't sure the light storyline and my attempted humor were going to come through for a reader. Special thanks to Nancy Mohr, who offered to look at my very rough first draft. Her e-mail the next day gave me the confidence to forge ahead. Her message, "When's the sequel?"

Thanks to my mother-in-law, Hildur, who delighted me with her story about going to a rural Minnesota funeral to hear the bagpipes. She didn't know the decedent or the family, but she reported that the pipers and church lunch were wonderful. She also suggested the recipe for canned green peas in lime Jello.

Following some rewrites, trusted proofreaders helped me through some technical and structural glitches. Thanks to Clem and Ann MacIlravie, Dennis Arnold, Wendy

Plauda, Miriam Milam, Frannie Brozo, Craig Kapfer, and my dog, Summer, (who listens patiently to my agonizing over plots and dialogue without complaint).

Very special thanks to Pat Morris for her skillful editing, subtle suggestions, encouragement, and support. She did not edit the acknowledgements, so do not blame her for the mistakes!

Thanks to Julie, my wife and sometimes the writing widow, for your love and support.